THE MYSTERIOUS BAKERY

ON

RUE DE PARIS

THE MYSTERIOUS BAKERY ON RUE DE PARIS

by Evie Gaughan

Copyright: 2014 Evie Gaughan

Find out more about the author and upcoming events online at www.eviegaughan.com

Prologue

The only thing worse than having a mid-life crisis is finding out about it from your Dad.

"Apparently the tell-tale signs are looking up ex-boyfriends on Facebook; dyeing your hair to cover the greys and the sudden desire to play a musical instrument," he rhymed off one morning, reading one of the dailies.

I would have scoffed and brushed it off, except I had been dyeing my hair Cherry Chestnut for some time now and just the other week my cousin and I had stalked my first boyfriend from school on Facebook. Granted, we were drunk, but it was on that same night that I vowed to take up the cello. I just had this ominous feeling that everything was passing me by and I was trying desperately to catch up. Yet it was only as I sat at the bus stop on the end of our road, quietly fidgeting with my handbag in that nervous habit of mine, that the realisation truly hit me. A man around my own age (i.e. the age when wearing comfortable shoes just makes more sense) came walking slowly by with a toddler, determined to make her own clumsy way down the street. I smiled, as if I knew what it must feel like to walk protectively behind your offspring, and he smiled back, revealing the kind of dimples a girl could swoon over. Yes, swoon. Just then the little girl let her concentration lapse and tumbled helplessly over her own uncooperative feet, resulting in a wail that would wake the dead. I moved to get up, but of course her father had instantly scooped her up into his capable arms, whispering soft reassurances into her red-hot ears. They plopped down beside me, their sudden proximity causing me to flush with awkwardness. I had no idea what to do or say – it seemed an intimate moment between father and child – until inspiration struck.

"Would you like a sweetie?" I asked, with all the vintage charm of a fifties housewife.

The crying halted instantly and a shy profile of a protruding lower lip and a curious, moistened eye turned to see what was on offer. I dug into my handbag with a force, and produced the roll of mints I always keep stocked. I could see the thought forming in her young mind… 'mints? Are you serious lady?' But she took one all the same, beggars can't be choosers after all.

"Now what do we say to the nice lady?" Her father prompted.

A muffled 'ank-u' ended our meeting and with another dazzling smile, her father swooped her up onto his shoulders and they continued on their merry way. I felt about 100 years old. I was the nice old lady who handed out mints… MINTS… to little children. A spinster who didn't even have the excuse of putting off having a family for a glittering career. A withering antique, dusty from lack of use and no longer relevant. That was the day I knew something had to change. That was the day I decided to go to Paris.

Chapter 1

The storm had really taken hold by the time I got to Dublin airport. A leaden sky lashed down rain onto the tarmac and buildings with a fury, as though the Gods themselves had something negative to say about my decision to leave.

"Paris? In France?"

"Yes Dad, we've been through this a million times, and I do wish you'd stop saying it as though it's the outer reaches of Mongolia." As I checked I had my passport for the umpteenth time, the trusty old Ford came to a halt outside Departures.

"I don't mean to Edie, it's just..." he hesitated, rubbing his early morning stubble and fixing his gaze on anything but me. "Are ya sure now?"

I wanted to scream – 'of course I'm not sure you bloody idiot, I'm scared shitless, but if it's a choice between sitting at home wondering 'what Mum would've done', and setting out into the complete unknown, the answer was simple.

"*Oui Papa,*" I replied in my thick Irish accent, producing a reluctant smile from his lips. "You're just put out because you won't have me popping in every day to do the housework," I cajoled. He smiled at that. "I'll be grand and so will you." Placing a quick kiss on his cheek, I pushed the door open to brave the elements and extricated my case from the boot.

I thought it would take all of my resolve not to look back, but a boisterous wind held no such sentiment and pushed me towards the glass doors, as if hastening my departure. Walking through the airport with people milling around like ducks in thunder (one of my Dad's old sayings), I felt truly cosmopolitan and significant, for the first time in years. Wearing my beige Mac that screamed sophistication and chocolate brown boots, I trailed my new hard case behind me with an exaggerated swagger of confidence. However, as the tannoy announced last calls and missing passengers for exotic locations such as Egypt and Singapore, something inside of me flip-flopped. Things started to become blurry around the edges and it became clear that I didn't know where I was going, or worse still, why. Thankfully a woman close to my own age, dressed in an emerald green uniform greeted me with an impossibly huge smile and asked to see my ticket.

"Oh lovely, you're off to Paris is it?" she said, as if people did this kind of thing everyday of the week. It never entered her head that some saddos had only been to an airport once, and that was a school trip to London.

I nodded dumbly, unable to verbalise any kind of reply.

"Right so, you're over here at the check in desk on the left," she said, guiding my arm like a nurse in a care home, "and enjoy the city of love!"

"Oh I, well yes okay," I finally found my bumbling voice, but she had already moved on to her next patient.

After a nice wander around the duty free, I had regained my composure somewhat. There was bound to be the odd moment of weakness, I assured myself. After all, I had spent most of my life living in the same area, seeing the same people and doing the same things. For the first time in my life, I was stepping outside of my comfort zone and it felt both exhilarating and terrifying. I had felt so confident answering the ad in the paper:-

Wanted: Shop manager for a quaint little bakery in Paris. Accommodation provided. English required.

It would hardly be Galeries Lafayette, but it was something I knew I could do despite the language barrier. My Leaving Certificate French left a lot to be desired, but I had been brushing up on my phrase book for the last few weeks and watching re-runs of Amélie. My daydreams were filled with visions of a chic, sophisticated *boulangerie* in one of the posh *quartiers* of Paris, modern but with a nod to vintage. Frankly I was surprised with how quickly I got the job, even without a proper interview. I couldn't quite believe my luck. A few quick-fire questions over the phone, ensuring my high level of spoken English and a background in the service industry, and that was it. My career path had been something of a cul-de-sac, in that I never really figured out what I wanted to do, so I just ended up waitressing. It was meant to be a temporary thing; a way to earn some money while I figured things out. But over time, my future became more and more unclear and my job was the only stable thing I had to hold on to. At the age of thirty-five, I just couldn't see myself doing anything else. Until Paris came calling.

While attempting to choose between a Mac blush and a liquid eyeliner, I heard a breathy young woman sing the announcement:

"Final call for passenger Edith Lane travelling to Paris on flight EI754 please proceed to gate 9 immediately, as the gate is now closing, thank you."

I grabbed both products and practically threw money at the shop assistant, making a dash for the flight. In true old Hollywood style, we had to walk across the tarmac to our plane, which had those moveable stairs wheeled up to the doorway. Passengers attempted to shield themselves from the swirling wind and rain with coats, scarves and newspapers – all failing miserably to do the job. Yet for me, the entire thing took on the romantic glow of a bygone era. A soundtrack of Louis Armstrong played in my ears, with a lazy trumpet announcing the beginning of my new life in France. As my fellow travellers climbed awkwardly up the damp steps to the plane, I imagined myself in a black and white movie, a sweeping romance with a Humphrey Bogart type seeing me off. 'Here's lookin' at you kid', I nodded to Dublin airport and turned to greet the air hostess like a long lost friend.

"What's your one grinnin' about?" I heard someone whisper behind me, but I didn't care. This was my great adventure and I intended to soak up every second of it. For years I had watched old films with my mother, sighing enviably at elegant actresses like Grace Kelly or Audrey Hepburn who embodied the kind of self-assured, fearless woman I hoped to be. Sitting in the back kitchen with my mother and listening to her old jazz records, just dreaming of the day when I would find the courage to be the star of my own movie brought back bittersweet memories. For when the time came for me to flee the nest, she needed me to stay. Not that she would ever have asked it of me, but it was natural as breathing, caring for her. Then those movies became our escape. Casablanca, High Society, Breakfast At Tiffany's and Roman Holiday created a world of timeless fantasy, satisfying both of our needs to live a life less ordinary. But there are some things in life you cannot escape, no matter how hard you wish it were so.

Sitting in my seat, as the rain lashed relentlessly against the oval window, I noticed a tall, silver-haired man scanning the aisles for his seat. There was something in his piercing blue eyes that caught my attention and I found myself hoping that he would take the seat beside me. It was Ryanair after all – no need to stand on ceremony around here. I tried to arrange my features into a nonchalant yet inviting look and to my great surprise, he smiled back and deftly swerved into the seat beside me. 'This is it', I thought to myself, 'This is the beginning of something amazing and we haven't even left the tarmac yet!'

He removed his coat, revealing a shocking white collar and a cross pinned to the breast of his shirt.

"Do you mind if I sit here?" he asked politely.

"No, not at all father," I sighed, breathless with disappointment. Oh well, at least God would be keeping an extra special eye on the plane. Which was just as well, for when we made our laboured ascent into the angry sky, I and my fellow passengers recited silent prayers several times over as our flying tin can lurched up and down in the turbulence. Babies cried, children whimpered and I anxiously sang 'Fly Me To The Moon' aloud, inwardly wondering why in God's name I had ever left the comfort of my parents' three bed semi in Dublin.

"Are you alright?" spoke the dapper priest at my side, startling me out of my fear-induced stupor.

"Oh, me? Yes of course, I'm grand," I assured him, undecidedly pleased to have a man of the cloth at my side.

"There's no need to worry at all," he continued, closing the Ken Bruen crime thriller he was reading. "I've read the end of this story, and we all arrive safely in the end."

This statement coupled with a mischievous wink made me laugh and automatically I relaxed a little.

"What takes you to Paris?" he enquired.

"I'm starting a new job, running a little bakery."

"Well that's very interesting. Isn't it amazing that they couldn't find someone in all of Paris to do that job?" he marvelled, shaking his head.

It struck me as most peculiar that this thought had never once entered my head and it irritated me no end that he was the one to spot such an obvious oversight. I smiled politely in agreement, but inside felt a mountain of doubts towering over my new life. What did I really know about where I was going? And why were they so quick to offer me a job without so much as an interview?

"Do you have family in Paris?" he interjected again, not finished with his interrogation.

"No, no family. Just going on my own," I replied in an upbeat tone that felt contrived.

"Aren't you the brave one," he said, winking again.

A flash of lightning lit the entire inside of the plane with a blinding spotlight, silencing everyone on board for a moment and then causing the children to cry even harder.

'We're all going to die!' I wanted to shout, but instead I bent forwards and cradled my head in my arms on the food tray.   I just kept whispering, 'Help me Mum, help me'. Within minutes, the captain's voice crackled over the intercom and assured everyone that all was well and we were now beginning our descent into Charles de Gaulle airport.

Chapter 2

So it wasn't the best start to my Parisian dream, but I was determined to put the doubts and travel sickness behind me. Charles De Gaulle airport proved a fascinating distraction, all curved glass ceilings and futuristic-looking glass tunnels carrying jaded passengers from one level to the other, like a giant hamster cage with tubes. It screamed style over practicality. 'How French,' I thought admiringly. Dragging my wheelie case behind me, my hair blowing in the cool, dry air-conditioning, I felt a million dollars. After forty minutes of an obstacle course, I felt less than half a million dollars, as it became clear I hadn't a clue where I was supposed to be going. I couldn't see a sign anywhere for Compiègne and the constant noise, people, announcements and general air of chaos did not help matters. All I really wanted to do was flop down on a comfortable chair and order my first cup of real French coffee, but I decided to be proactive and call Madame Moreau – my future French employer at the Bakery.

"*Âllo?*" came a croaky old voice.

I recalled the line I had been practising and responded, "Um, *oui* hello, eh *bonjour* Madame Moreau... eh, *ici* Edith Lane?" I planned on ending every sentence with a question, as in 'Do you understand me?' Even though I had spent the last few weeks cramming with French language tapes, my 'helpful phrases' felt painfully inadequate in this situation.

"*Que voulez-vous?*"

"Yes well, *je suis* at the airport and um, *je ne connais pas* how to get to Compiègne?" My voice wavered as the woman at the end of the line sounded decidedly unwelcoming and I had the uncontrollable urge to weep. 'Get it together Edie', I urged myself silently.

"*Ah, vous êtes la fille qui va travailler dans la boulangerie, c'est ça?*"

"*Oui*, yes, I'm Edith from Ireland, *Irlandaise!*" I sighed with relief at her recognition of my name. After talking to that doubting Thomas on the plane, I was starting to worry if all of this was a hoax.

"*Vous devez aller à la Gare Du Nord et vous prenez le train à Compiègne, d'accord? A plus tard alors.*"

The line went dead.

"Eh hello? *Âllo*, Madame Moreau? *Je ne comprends pas*, I don't know what part of Paris you're in. Hello?" And that was that. 'What a rude old cow', I thought with indignation. 'Well that's a fine welcome to the city of love'. Refusing to be deterred, I approached a young woman at what seemed to be an information desk, but could equally have been a car hire booth – I was beyond caring.

"*Bonjour Madame, puis-je vous aider?*" she began politely, though I wondered how long that would last.

"Do you speak English by any chance? I need directions and I don't want to make any mistakes." I explained.

"Of course Madame, 'ow can I 'elp?" She smiled sincerely.

"Well, I need to get to Compiègne, I think it's a district in Paris somewhere."

"I'm sorry Madame, but ze only Compiègne near 'ere is one hour north of Paris."

"It's Mademoiselle actually," I pointed out, slightly miffed at the presumption. Then her words sank in. "Sorry, did you say one hour north of Paris? No, there must be some mistake. I'm here to take up my position in the Boulangerie et Pâtisserie de Compiègne… in Paris," I asserted.

"I can show you, if you like Madame, excuse me, Mademoiselle," she continued, turning a computer screen so I could see a map of Paris and its outskirts. Far to the north lay the town of Compiègne. "See, it is in the ze department of Oise, in ze region of Picardy and by train, ze best way to arrive at Compiègne is to take le RER B to La Gare Du Nord, see? *Vous voyez là*?" she asked, pointing to the map.

"*Oui, je vois*, yes," I whispered in response, with a sinking feeling in my stomach. That was what Mme Moreau had said, La Gare Du Nord. I wasn't going to be living and working in Paris at all. And if that wasn't true, what else had I been misled about? The helpful young woman continued and even wrote everything down, as I must have looked completely lost. And besides, what was a department when it was at home?

"*Alors*, ze trains depart every 15 minutes and *ze* ticket is nine euros and fifty cents," she said, writing the information down with a flourish of her manicured hand. "I wish you a good journey Madame."

I was caught in a stare, eyes focussed on the map of a strange town outside Paris, full of odd street names and road numbers.

"It's Mademoiselle," I croaked and headed straight for the nearest bathroom. Looking at myself in the mirror, I saw a very sorry sight indeed. The rotund chignon I had forced my hair into this morning had completely unravelled, the dark circles I had concealed with my expensive Mac purchase at the airport reappeared like moon shadows under my eyes and my cracked lips betrayed my doubt as they began to tremble.

"Look, you're a grown woman; get a hold of yourself!" I shouted, giving myself a quick smack on the cheek. Wrong move; that just left me feeling sad and bullied.

"Right, different approach. Okay, no-one said this was going to be easy," I assured myself, like an audio self-help book. "Every heroine must face her obstacles and that's all this is, an obstacle." Talking in such a positive tone began to calm me down and I reached for some tissue to start rebuilding the façade of confidence with makeup. "So I won't be living a glamourous life in Paris," I mumbled, "but this Compiègne place is only an hour away, and who knows, maybe it's the most picturesque town in France." That was the spirit, and besides, how would it look if I gave up on my big adventure before I even left the airport? Just then a woman stepped out of one of the cubicles, giving me a wary look.

"Oh, never mind me, just talking to myself!" I joked, and received a stony-faced glare for my troubles. I was obviously a major hit with the French.

I left the airport with renewed vigour and congratulated myself on the ease with which I found the RER B train for the Gare Du Nord. We trundled along the outskirts of Paris at a healthy pace and finally as the suburbs gave way to the city, I felt as though I had truly arrived. I was taken aback by the beauty of the architecture, the scale of everything dwarfing anything I had seen in Dublin. Monuments gilded with gold, fountains splashing generously and red, white and blue flags flying proudly on every building. My heart pounded with anticipation and excitement. The adventure was once again afoot.

Arriving at Gare Du Nord, a fresh bout of confusion set in as I tried to make sense of the signs. I was improving, when it came to figuring out where the hell I was going, and picked up a map at the information desk. I figured I had earned a well-deserved rest before the next leg of my journey and so I hauled myself onto a stool at a kiosk in the grand station. Ordering my first real French coffee, I toyed with the idea of ordering a croissant. It wasn't so much that I was minding my figure, although carbs usually meant exercise, so I tended to avoid both. But lately, I had just lost my appetite for certain things, and the rather tired looking basket of dark brown croissants did nothing to alter that. Burned croissants aside, I audibly sighed with content as the dark, robust coffee filled my taste buds with a smooth, dark chocolaty warmth. Like caffeinated magic, it lifted my spirits too and I realised, I was having a coffee in Paris! Albeit in a train station, but it was a train station in Paris. It felt so romantic. All that was missing was some Edith Piaf bellowing over the loudspeakers, instead it was some awful British pop group.

Finally, it was time to head towards my final destination and I deftly boarded the train on the Paris - Saint-Quentin line to Compiègne. I found a seat by the window, though by this stage the sky was growing dark and as the train pulled away from the station, the lights of Paris blinked a luminous farewell.

Chapter 3

The sky was completely dark by the time the train pulled into Compiègne station. I felt tired and hungry as I pulled on my coat and prepared to step once more into the unknown. Alighting the train, I noticed a young boy of about 15 sitting on one of the two benches adorning the platform. He was engrossed in some sort of computer game and it was only when the wheels of my case announced my presence, did he look up from under his hoodie.

"*Pardon Madame*?" he shouted.

My instincts told me he was someone to be avoided, so I pretended I hadn't heard and continued on my way.

"*Pardon, êtes-vous Madame Lane*?" he persisted.

"Oh, yes. I mean *oui*. And you are?"

"*Je m'appelle Manu. Madame Moreau m'a envoyé vous chercher.*"

Already he had taken the handle of my case and was leaving the station.

"But, wait, I…" my words bounced off his heedless back. That was it; I'd had enough. I was tired, hungry and fed up with being treated like a nobody in this country.

"Oi, kid, you listen to me right? I've been travelling all day to get here, nearly went down in a thunder storm in the process, so I think the least you can do is address me like a civilised human being and tell me exactly where we are going, instead of herding me there like a lost sheep!" There, that felt so good and I was certain that I had left him in no doubt as to the cut of my jib.

He just turned casually and simply said, "*La boulangerie*," as if it was the most obvious thing in the world, which in fact it was. He gave a little signal with his hand that I should follow and set off once again with my brand new suitcase rolling behind him.

"And just so you know, it's Mademoiselle dammit!" I finished, determined to have the last word.

I finally caught up with my hooded guide as we entered an old cobbled street. The place seemed deserted and a million miles away from my Parisian dream. Still, it did have an old-world appeal and despite the cold and the dark, I did my utmost to feel optimistic about what lay ahead. 'A hot cup of tea and everything will seem better', I reassured myself. We walked along by a river lined with benches and manicured trees, and crossed by ornate bridges leading to who knew where. I couldn't imagine ever feeling at home or familiar with this place and if I had a dog, I would have told him we weren't in Dublin anymore. Turning a corner, I was surprised to see a street full of wooden frame houses, like something out of Tudor England. The old section of the town was like a fairy-tale village and I half expected the walls to be made of gingerbread. Nothing seemed to have a right angle and dormer windows peeped out of crooked roofs with pointy hats on.

"*Ici,*" my guide announced curtly.

Overhead I saw a sign saying 'La Boulangerie et Pâtisserie de Compiègne', while on the corner of the building was a small sign with the street name, 'Rue de Paris. Oh how I rued my ignorance.

"Well, it's exactly what it says on the tin then; a bakery on the road to Paris."

"*Comment?*" Manu drawled, as if the effort of speaking to a boring, middle-aged woman was too much of a drain on his time.

"Nothing, forget it, or what is it again... *Laisse tomber?*"

Something between a grunt and a sniff was all I got in return. He had a key and opened the glass-panelled door to the bakery. I could feel my excitement return at the prospect of seeing my new 'career' in France. At first I noticed the floor tiles – exquisitely ornate and designed in peacock blue and gold, with hints of bright orange at the centre. The counter was plain, but functional and of course empty at the end of the day. The shop was just large enough to accommodate three typically French bistro tables and chairs, all located by the large front window looking onto the street.

A large art nouveau style mirror with a gilt gold frame took up the entirety of one wall from floor to ceiling, creating the illusion of a grander space. Sconces lit the honey coloured walls with a dim light and as my eyes adjusted, I found myself suddenly confronted with a sturdy looking woman dressed in a black skirt to the knee and a matching cardigan that fought admirably to contain her large bosom. Grey hair framed a sour face that held the echoes of kindness long since departed. Despite myself, I instinctively took a step back.

"Madame Lane," she announced in a way that wasn't really a question or a statement.

"Mmhmm, *je suis*, well it's Mademoiselle actually," I floundered. Her deep-set brown eyes were formidable, despite her short stature.

"*Venez, je vais vous montrer votre chambre.*"

With that, she padded silently behind the counter to an open doorway and began climbing some rather steep looking stairs. I turned around to thank Manu, but he had already left.

"Welcome to France Edith," I muttered, picking up my suitcase.

Following Mme Moreau up the stairs, I began to feel like Alice In Wonderland. I juggled unsuccessfully with my

19

suitcase as it knocked off the narrow walls and in the end resorted to carrying it over my head. The stairs took a dangerous 90 degree turn and then quite suddenly, I found myself in my studio apartment. The term attic would have been a generous one in describing my new home. At the nearest end of the oblong room a day bed sat snugly in front of an unlit stove and to my right was a kitchenette consisting of an electric hob and a sink with a tiny shelf above for delph. At the far end of the room stood a giant oak wardrobe taking up far more space than was practical and behind a screen was what I assumed to be the WC.

"*Voilà,*" Mme Moreau announced as though mightily pleased with her lodgings.

I was literally speechless, but she took this to mean quiet bliss. With a gruff '*Bonne nuit*' and orders to be up for seven, she took her leave and left me to my doll's house. I flung my case on the bed and myself along with it, where I sat motionless for a long time. My phone announced the arrival of a text message, rousing me from my mini coma. Dad, of course. Checking to see if I got to France in one piece. I texted him that I had arrived safe and was just settling into my lovely new home. Somehow, this little fib gave me strength to get back on my feet, unpack and set about making the space my own. I was used to making the most of small spaces and while I had hoped this journey was leading me to bigger and better things (karma demanded it!), I assured myself that great things start with small beginnings.

***

I had a fitful sleep that night and woke to some strange noises in the building. I put this down to the creaking timbers and fell back into strange dreams that were vivid and disturbing. My mother, as always, was there and we were on a ship trying to get somewhere. At some point I lost her and spent the dream searching frantically over all the decks. I awoke to the sound of low whimpering, then realised the strangled noise was coming from my throat. The alarm on my phone rang soon after to announce the dawn of my first morning in Paris. It was six o'clock and already I could smell the scent of warm bread wafting up the stairs. It hadn't occurred to me the night before to ask where the actual ovens were. Still, today would be my first official working day and I figured I would discover all the inner workings of the place soon enough.

The attic, or should I say atelier if you want to sound artsy about it, was bloody freezing. My nose felt as though it had spent the night at the North Pole, and my toes along with it. In fact all of my extremities were in serious danger of frost bite. Insulation was obviously a foreign concept over here, so I set to lighting the little stove with a bundle of wood stored in a basket at its side. Fifteen minutes later, after filling the room with eye-watering clouds of smoke, I admitted defeat and instead turned on the little portable electric hob to heat my coffee pot and the room. I danced briskly on the chilly floorboards as I pulled on some woolly tights and flower print dress. Some might say (my father being one of them) that January was perhaps not the ideal time to start a new life abroad, and feeling the chills running down my spine, I had to agree. But Mme Moreau was quite insistent that she needed a manager to start immediately, which now made me wonder what had happened to the previous manager.

Chapter 4

I gingerly made my way down the stairs for a quarter to seven. Mme Moreau was already piling every size and shape of baguette, loaf and roll into wicker baskets behind the counters. The smell was intoxicating. The warm loaves filled the air with a slightly sweet and robustly fragrant scent, like a warm, doughy hug. I ignored my salivating mouth and straightened my dress before I greeted Mme Moreau.

"*Tiens,*" was all she said, handing me a navy check apron.

"*Merci,*" I replied chirpily, deciding to perceive her taciturn, monosyllabic approach as a challenge. My Everest, if you will.

"Madame Moreau, I was wondering if I would be able to see the ovens at some stage, you know, see where all the magic happens." I'm not sure why, but I used jazz hands to convey my excitement.

The look I received then can only be described as disdain mixed with a good dollop of annoyance.

"You 'ave no business going downstairs, ever."

I was quite shocked to hear her reply in English. I knew she spoke some English, the ad in the paper had said so, when it explained how popular Compiègne was among tourists. But choosing that statement as her first in my own language made it clear she meant it to be understood. No going downstairs.

"Of course, no problem. I just thought it might be nice to…"

"*Non!*" she bellowed, her dark eyes fixing me with a stare that turned my blood cold.

"*Non*, okay, I got it," I said, like a sulky child.

"*Écoutez, Édith,*" she began in a more conciliatory tone "ze Boulanger, 'e is *très* particular about who is going in his kitchen, *hein*? Is better if you are 'ere to manage the shop, non?" she said, nodding.

Unfortunately, Francophiles have no 'th' in their language and so I was still hung up on the fact that she had just called me 'Edeet'.

"*Édith, vous comprenez?*"

"Huh? Oh yes, right, got it. Grumpy baker, do not disturb," I spoke slowly as I copied the words in my notebook.

"What is *zis*?" Mme Moreau asked, looking curiously at my notebook.

"Well it's where I keep my notes. You see I like to write everything down so if I forget anything, I can refer to it, um, here." Her bemused look was quite confusing. I mean what did the old curmudgeon want? I was being professional. "And for orders, people will be placing orders, won't they?"

At this she began to grin, a not altogether unpleasant grin, but it held the kind of mischief that made me nervous.

"*Ma pauvre*, you will 'ave little time for writing notes," she cackled and continued stacking bread into baskets.

I couldn't imagine how a little bakery in a small provincial town would be over-run with customers, but I decided to keep my thoughts to myself. Just then Manu appeared at the front door looking far more alert and groomed than he had the previous evening. After a chorus of *bonjours*, he set about loading boxes of bread on a small scooter just outside in a tower that seemed to defy gravity. Seeing my inquisitive glance, Mme Moreau informed me that Manu was in charge of deliveries to local hotels and restaurants. Despite the old fashioned look of the place, their business seemed to be organised and profitable enough to keep at least four employees in earnings.

She gave me my first job of filling the glass counter to the side of the serving counter full of mouth-watering pâtisseries. First I began with the classic *pain au chocolats* and croissants, which sat in large baskets on top. Then I placed two large round flans, bright and yellow like the sun on the bottom shelf at the front along with a *tarte tatin*. The middle shelf was for savouries such as *croque-madame* and *croque-monsieur* and pizza cut into squares, which left the top shelf for tempting treats like éclairs filled with fresh cream, fruit tarts glazed with apricot syrup, and not forgetting those little scallop-shaped *madeleines*. Everything looked so wonderfully appealing; I could understand the old adage of eating with your eyes.

At seven am sharp, Mme Moreau turned the '*ouvert*' sign and opened the bakery for business. To my surprise, there were a handful of customers already standing by the door and she greeted them with an easy charm I wouldn't have thought possible a moment before. I braced myself for my first French customer, mildly confident that I had enough mastery of the basics to see myself through. Wrong! The first gentleman to approach the counter gave his order so quickly that all I heard was '*Bonjour*' and caught nothing else.

"*Um, pardonnez-moi?*" was all I could manage in a voice that sounded embarrassingly pathetic to my own ears.

"*Je prends deux croissants et une baguette, s'il vous plaît,*" he repeated, but he may as well have not bothered. I was painfully unprepared for the speed at which the customers spoke, their regional accent or their slang. For the first time, and unfortunately with an audience, I realised that this had been a big mistake. Huge. I wanted to just run out of there and never look back. Somehow, Mme Moreau must have read my thoughts and rather gracefully introduced me to her patrons as Edeet from England. On any other occasion that slip-up would have warranted a very patriotic comeback, but I was floundering and she was offering me a life-line. They all seemed to ooh and ahh at the revelation of a foreigner in their midst, and I did my best impression of a 'lovely girl competition' entrant, smiling and nodding dumbly. We worked out that simply pointing was the best means of communication until my French improved and for the most part, it began to work out quite well.

I had underestimated La Boulangerie et Pâtisserie de Compiègne, as the shop held a steady flow of customers all through the morning. However at lunchtime, which I found out was noon in this part of the world, the place was jumping. I worked alongside Mme Moreau who kept a furious pace, as the line wormed its way out the door. I had not yet been entrusted with the coffee machine, but I was now making short work of the cash register that mercifully resembled a straightforward calculator. Our own lunch-time finally arrived at 2pm when I was informed that the bakery closed from 2pm to 4 pm daily. At first I felt a little dismayed at having to spend two hours in my cramped attic alone, but on balance I figured a bite to eat and a little nap might just be ideal. That was when it dawned on me that I had to do some grocery shopping. My little kitchenette cupboards were almost entirely bare, so I grabbed my coat and started off down the road in search of a *supermarché*.

The afternoon had turned into one of those bright winter days where it almost dazzles the eyes to look up. All I had seen of the town so far was the brisk walk from the station to the bakery, which was a muddled night-time view of cobbled streets, closed shutters and little else. But walking out onto the street in the daytime lifted my heart in a way I didn't think possible. It felt like being transported onto a movie set; every clichéd idea I had about a French town was here. Now the natives weren't wearing berets or striped tops with garlic tied around their necks, but they just had an air of self-importance and sophistication. And even though the women were dressed quite casually and not in haute couture, their sense of style truly set them apart from their European cousins. However the smoking rate, especially among the teenagers, was alarming. 'Think of your teeth!' I wanted to shout at the younger girls, but then I vaguely remembered what it was like to be so young that you felt invincible and I kept my advice to myself.

Not to be outdone on the fashion stakes, I pulled the collar of my expensive cream coat up against the chilly breeze and set off once again. Our cobbled street was home to a host of other distinctively French establishments. A traditional Crêperie with a similar timber façade to the bakery held an enviable position on the corner of three streets, followed by a *Tabac* (or a newsagents for all intents and purposes) and a *salon de thé*, or a tea room. Looking at this street, it was easy to imagine that the French had nothing better to do than sit around indulging their appetites. However, it seemed that we were not the only ones taking a long lunch – everywhere was shut. It was remarkable to see how our cultures differed – these kinds of shenanigans would be unthinkable back home.

I wandered along, taking turns here and there, wandering past a picture-postcard scene of a group of old men playing *boules* or *pétanque* in a beautiful park named Parc de Songeons. Everything had such a laconic feel to it, the trees swaying in the breeze, the men having a good natured argument about whose ball was the biggest, or the closest probably. Turning right past the river, I found myself in the more modern part of the town where brasseries buzzed with patrons sitting outside, soaking up the atmosphere. It was like coming out of a time warp to see banks, offices and bustling traffic, and for some reason, it felt a little overwhelming. The smart pale stone facades with white shutters seemed full of their own importance and a little too perfect. I found a little Monoprix supermarket and was completely spoiled for choice when it came to fresh produce like cheese and fruit, but other staples were a little more difficult to track down. The closest thing I could get to proper tea was English breakfast tea and the milk situation was so confusing, I ended up leaving without any. I worked my way back to the Rue De Paris and had a curious look at the exterior door on the eastern side of the building that led to the basement where the ovens were. The street was on a slope and while the basement door was visible at the side of the building, the shop front was at street level at the front. The door was painted a deep blue and secured with a decorative lock and bolt that must have been an antique. It looked as though no-one had ever used that entrance and I began to wonder how on earth ingredients got in or bread got out. Surely everything didn't go through the shop? There was no time to investigate, as my stomach was so empty it growled. I let myself in through the shop and up the stairs to my atelier.

Chapter 5

Back in my little crooked house I enjoyed a very French lunch of brie, grapes and some weird kind of crackers, washed down with a very un-French (and un-Irish) black tea. I could hear noises in the apartment below me and began to wonder if that was indeed where Mme Moreau lived. I hadn't presumed to ask the night before and she was not exactly a woman to shower you with information. I flopped down on my sofa/bed and tried once again to make friends with the strange sausage-shaped structure that passed for a pillow in this country. I pondered over my first few hours in France, which frankly, felt like a lifetime. That's what happens when you are out of your comfort zone – time stretches like an elastic band, prolonging your discomfort and unease, accentuating your isolation. Had I expected a grumpy old woman for a boss and a matchbox for a home when I had answered that ad all those months ago? Did I really think that plonking myself in a foreign country would erase all the painful memories of the last eighteen months? Was I deluding myself that a dream to live in Paris (that I'd held since the age of six thanks to my aunt Gemma buying me a snow globe with the Eiffel tower) could really make me happy at the age of thirty-five? Every thought in my head was telling me what an idiot I had been and that leaving now would be smarter than prolonging the agony. But my heart wouldn't let me; despite the frosty welcome and the downright idiocy of acting on a childhood whim, my heart was holding out for something amazing to happen. And who was I to stand in the way of that?

***

I worked diligently all afternoon, growing in confidence with every new customer. Sure enough, there were quite a few tourists looking for what they had claimed was 'the best sourdough bread in all of France'. One American informed me that that's what it said in all the unofficial guidebooks. "It's a secret," he said, putting his index finger to his lips. I wasn't sure that that was such a good idea for business and suggested to Mme Moreau that it should be in the official guide books, but as per usual, she just scoffed at me, as though I was a little puppy who had just soiled the floor. It was a relief to speak to people in English after a long day of broken French and improvised sign language.

"So what brings you to Compiègne?" I asked an English husband and wife who stopped for a coffee and some éclairs.

"Oh we live here," said the woman, taking off her coat and sliding into the seat by the window.

"Really? Me too!" I replied, over eager to meet some fellow Anglophones.

"Yeah, we retired over here a few years ago from Bristol. Well, I say retired, I'm working part time as a tour guide, mostly for war buffs coming to see the Armistice Memorial," said the man, tucking heartily into his chocolate covered éclair. "Have you seen it yourself?" the wife asked.

"No actually, I've only been here for, ooh, 24 hours!" I replied.

This provoked a conversation I was to have many times over the next few months, involving lots of 'what brought you here's and 'was it a man?' to which I honestly replied, 'I couldn't say.'

"So what is the... Armistice, did you say?" I asked once the interrogation had ended.

"Well it's one of the most important sites in France regarding both World Wars," the man began, obviously a seasoned veteran of such things. "The Allies signed the Armistice with the Germans in World War One in a train carriage in the Forest of Compiègne. In 1940, the French signed an Armistice with Nazi Germany in the same clearing, Hitler's way of humiliating his enemies. It's really very interesting, you should visit if you're going to be staying here a while." He paused long enough to take a long gulp of his coffee. "My name's Geoff and this is Ruby," he said, handing me his card.

"And the château Geoff, don't forget the château!" piped Ruby.

"Oh wow, there's a castle here?"

"Well it is France love," said Geoff, bemused by my ignorance.

"Never mind him Edith, he's a proper know it all," Ruby said, swatting her husband on the arm. But if you don't mind me asking, what brought you here, or rather, how did you know you wanted to come to Compiègne?"

"I didn't," I replied flatly, "I thought I was coming to Paris".

***

As the evening rush died down and all the residents of Compiègne set off home with their baguettes in hand, Manu returned to help shut up shop. Like most teenagers, he had few words for anyone, but there was an obvious bond between himself and Mme Moreau. She never had to tell him what to do for he was industriously following a time-honoured routine they had forged long before my arrival. As for myself, my feet were burning with pain from standing all day, but I wouldn't give anyone the satisfaction of seeing me take a break. I could tell from both of their attitudes towards me that they didn't expect the foreigner to last very long and despite myself, I was inclined to agree.

I lifted all of the chairs onto the tables and began mopping the brightly tiled floor as Mme Moreau counted in the money in the till. To my complete astonishment, Manu spoke to me in barely audible tones.

"*Ça va?*" he said, lifting his head and casting a glance around the bakery, as if to say 'are you settling in okay?'

His simple show of kindness almost brought me to tears and I had to use all my will to stave off the stinging drops, wiping my eyes as though from tiredness.

"Ça va, I think," I smiled lopsidedly.

And with that, he hopped up, poured himself a large glass of water from the tap behind the counter and gulped it down in one go.

"*J'y vais,*" he said, taking more boxes with him and once again piling them on the scooter outside.

"Does he make deliveries, I mean, *livraisons* at this time of night?" I asked Mme Moreau as she locked the door behind him, the clock just striking eight.

Instead of just answering the question like a normal person, my new boss had a way of making you feel like an idiot for having asked it in the first place.

"*Non.*"

'Right, understood, or *bien compris* as you say here. Do not ask ridiculous questions you foreign simpleton,' I mumbled cleaning the glass shelves below the counter, when she appeared suddenly beside me, like a ghost.

"He delivers to the church Mademoiselle Édith, *pour les gens SDF, Sans Domicile Fixé.*" To my blank stare, she added "people who 'ave no place to live." With that irritated response, she shut the lights off and threatened to see me at the same time tomorrow morning.

"Oh yes Dad, the people here are just so welcoming and I've really hit it off with the owner, Mme Moreau," I told my father later that evening on the phone. In a strange way, it felt kind of nice making up the French dream I had expected to have before I got here and I was so good at it, I almost believed it myself.

Chapter 6

The following morning began much as the one before; Mme Moreau stacking the hot, crusty baguettes into baskets, me piling the golden, flaky pastries on the counter and the sweets in the glass display, while Manu packed his boxes for delivery. It still felt strange to be transplanted into this completely different environment, but less so than the day before. At least now I knew what to expect when the doors opened and the regulars poured in. Although trying not to eat the pastries was still a challenge. The aroma of hot baked goods was beginning to drive my insides wild with anticipation of a cheeky nibble at a *pain au chocolat* or an almond croissant. Mme Moreau however, seemed oblivious to the temptations that surrounded us. Still stubbornly clipped in her dealings with me, she oozed personality with her customers. Of course I couldn't understand all of what was said, but it was obvious she was something of a neighbourhood character - always with a sharp quip to throw her opponent off-guard and a wit and intellect to rival any French philosopher. This made me keenly aware of the fact that she and I were polar opposites. I tried too hard to make people like me and for the amount of time I succeeded in this endeavour, it hardly made all the effort worthwhile. Yet this cantankerous old dame had everyone eating out of her hand.

On the plus side, I was beginning to pick up some charming phrases while dealing with the customers like, *'Je vous en prie'*, which literally meant 'I beg you', but it seemed to be used as more of a 'you're welcome' or 'oh it was nothing' kind of phrase. It was interesting how, if you heard a phrase used enough times in the same situation, you kind of construed your own meaning, without the need to consult a phrase book. My accent was still frightfully clunky, like a pair of steel toe boots clod-hopping over all of their delicate phrases, but the customers seemed to appreciate the efforts I made.

Before closing at two, it was announced that I was to have the afternoon off. That was how Mme Moreau operated; she made things known, rather than telling you straight to your face. Apparently two days spent in France without the proper papers was two days too long.

"*Il faut aller à la Préfecture pour chercher votre Carte de Séjour,*" Manu advised, in a failed attempt to make things clearer.

"I have to go where to get my what now?" I asked, squinting my eyes in an attempt to understand.

Mme Moreau hefted herself onto the stool in the kitchen just behind us, showing for the first time, some signs of her age. She looked tired and it was clear by the way she rubbed wrists that there was a stiffness there.

"It is a Residence Card. If you are living in France for more than three months, you must *'ave* one."

Three months? I wasn't sure if I was going to last three days, but I wasn't about to argue with an afternoon off. After all, how hard could filling out a few forms be? Wrong again! After spending the best part of an hour trying to find the right building, (which was eventually marked out by its grey walls and grey people) I waited two hours in an unending queue of foreign students, immigrants and a lot of tired and forlorn looking people, only to be informed that the office closed at 4:30pm. The receptionist, a kind enough woman with an obsession for bangles, loaded my arms with half a rainforests' worth of paper and informed me that the office would re-open at 8:45am the following morning. I spent another three hours in a cafe trying to make sense of everything I needed, with four strong coffees and a dictionary. I ended up with a list that looked something like this:

· Passport
· Birth Certificate
· Attestation de Residence (Proof of Residency)
· Attestation de Bourse (Proof of Income)
· Timbre Fiscal (Some special stamp that, quite frankly, sounded makey-uppy)
· E111 Health Insurance
· 4 Passport Photos
· Self-Addressed Envelope
· Photocopies of all of the above

I can't say my enthusiasm for form-filling to remain in a country that obviously did not relish my presence was at an all-time high. But when it became clear that a Carte de Séjour was the key to opening a bank account and actually getting paid, I returned to the bakery and diligently searched out all of the documents I needed.

The following morning, after assuring Mme Moreau that I would only be gone for an hour, tops, I returned to Préfecture just as the doors opened. With only a handful of people ahead of me, I got to see someone within the half hour. A balding middle-aged man, who insisted on speaking to the empty space above my head, barely greeted me and proceeded to rifle through my carefully gathered documents. I discovered that the Préfecture was like the Council Office and the staff in this country were no different to the ones back home. Everything took an ice age to complete. His rather large belly prevented him from getting too close to his desk, so his outstretched arms shuffled the papers in a lazy manner that made it clear he felt this job was beneath him. In fact, I imagined his only pleasure was in using his limited position of power to make other people miserable. So I kept a neutral face, as if getting this card didn't matter to me one way or the other. We were playing Carte de Séjour poker. But as soon as he placed a fat hand on my birth certificate, his features betrayed his mirth. He had his ace.

"*On a besoin d'une traduction, Mademoiselle*," he said triumphantly.

Traduction, what the hell was that? "*Comment*?"

"*En français*," he replied at volume, as though speaking to an imbecile.

"*Mais*, how do I get one of those?" I fumed. "*Où*?"

"*Vous devez contacter l'Ambassade de France dans votre pays*," he said, dismissing me. And just like that, Caesar had turned his thumb downward and I was once again sent packing.

"You mean I have to contact the French Embassy in Dublin and get them to translate my birth cert? You've got to be joking!" I said, giving up on trying to argue with him in his own language. "And what about being a member of the happy-clappy EU? Doesn't that mean free movement between countries? I mean, I didn't even have to show my passport at the airport!" I lied.

But I could see that my anger had no effect on this man, in fact he probably enjoyed it. It was the only fun he had in his boring job. So I took back all of my papers in disgust and made as much racket as I could on the way out.

After hours spent making phone calls home, faxing documents back and forth and generally getting nowhere, I arrived back at the bakery just in time for lunch. To say Mme Moreau was unimpressed was an understatement. I flopped down at one of the tables and buried my head in my arms. Why did everything in this country have to be such a battle? I just stayed there, in the empty bakery, feeling sorry for myself. Something tugged at the back of my mind; a desire of some sort that I couldn't quite put my finger on. I lifted my head and looked in the direction of the pastry counter. Mme Moreau had covered mostly everything, except for a fat, golden croissant that sat solitary in a rectangular basket. Like I said, up to that point, my appetite was lack lustre, but the sight of that plain croissant against the gingham serviette made my mouth salivate. I hungered for it. In an instant, I was at the counter, ripping it apart and dipping it into a dish of softened butter. The flaky pastry stuck to my fingers like buttery confetti and the soft interior brought utter joy to my mouth. I groaned involuntarily with the pleasure of tasting that sweet, succulent croissant, dripping with butter. I felt like a woman possessed. It was as though the pastry was unlocking something within me. I felt wild and free and like I just didn't care about anything. I started to question if there weren't some kind of barbiturates in the dough, such was the effect. I uncovered the other baskets and fished out a *pain au chocolat* and an almond croissant for myself. I made a giant *café au lait* for myself and spent the next half hour indulging in my new-found appetite. I licked my fingers, slurped my coffee and only when I leaned back into my chair, spent after my indulgence, did I realise that it was almost time to open the shop again.

After a long and busy afternoon at work, I decided to go for a walk around the '*quartier*' to breathe the cool, crisp evening. It did my heart and soul good to get out and about after such a frustrating day. The streets were lit up by elegant street lamps that curled like a shepherd's crook. Compiègne's picturesque thoroughfares certainly held their charm, but I felt so far from home and pathetically alone. This whole following your dreams thing was not at all how I had imagined it. Where were all the fun friends I was supposed to meet, the fun experiences I was supposed to be having? I watched enough movies to know what should be happening when you chase after your heart's desire, but none of that big screen magic seemed to be happening here. It was just boring, lonely and a bit scary. Everything that had happened since the plane touched down in Charles De Gaulle only confirmed my suspicions that coming here was a big mistake.

I passed by a hairdressers on the busy Rue Solferino and saw a photo of a very French-looking model (surprise, surprise) sporting a gamine hairdo. Her hair colour, a kind of dark chestnut, was quite similar to my own. Yet while my long shapeless do lacked any kind of style, her cropped 'Audrey Hepburn' homage was the essence of chic. 'Well if you can't beat them, join them', I thought to myself, determined not to let my doubts get the better of me. Maybe it wasn't 'La vie en rose' just yet, but I was giving my dreams a shot, and that had to count for something.

Chapter 7

On my one week anniversary, I decided to treat myself, so when the bakery shut for lunch, I grabbed my coat and headed straight for the hairdressers. It was a short walk from the cobbled Rue De Paris and onto a very modern and trendy Rue de Solferino. I felt a little less intimidated by my unfamiliar surroundings and found myself admiring the smart shop fronts and their stylish patrons. However, as I walked into the salon, I was again transported to another era. The decor was a retro nod to the fifties, with the entire salon painted with bright, ice-cream pastels of pink, peach and cream. To the right was a nail bar with stools that looked for all the world like they had been stolen from an American diner. The rest of the salon was similarly kitted out with white leather styling chairs and pink-framed mirrors. I half expected them to set my hair in rollers with a polka dot scarf round my head. A glamorous woman with a peroxide blonde bouffant, that would not have looked out of place on Marilyn Monroe, approached me with red talons and made me retreat.

"*Bonjour Mademoiselle,*" she welcomed me in a sing-songy voice, red lips grinning.

"*Bonjour*, I um.. I'm not sure," I hesitated, pleased that for once someone spotted I wasn't married and didn't assume that at my age I should be.

"*Ah, vous êtes anglaise? Pas de problème – ma fille parle un peu anglais,*" she explained, followed by a banshee wail of "*Nicole! Viens ici.*"

I smiled politely and took the seat she pointed to. In her best English she manufactured the words "Just one moment pleeese," with the most adorable accent I had ever heard.

Nicole's entrance caused my jaw to drop – I had never seen anything like her. Her curves had been poured into a black and white polka dot dress and she wore a red scarf tied neatly around her neck. Her hair was jet black and styled in a simple pony tail with a quiff at the front. The words Betty and Boop came to mind.

"Hello, my name is Nicole," she said, stretching her hand out.

I fumbled to look less star-struck by her and failed miserably. "I just love your look," I said sincerely. "And I'm Irish by the way. My name is Edith, but please call me Edie because everyone pronounces my name in a way that makes it sound like 'edit' or 'eejit' and I can't bear either." I realised I was babbling, but Nicole just smiled.

"I don't think you want to do that," she grinned, "with the accent on the E, people will start to call you 'Eddie'!"

We both laughed as if we'd known each other forever and for the first time since boarding the plane, I felt as though I could let my guard down.

"How long 'ave you been in France?" she asked as she deftly lifted my hair and placed a gown around my shoulders. A coffee also appeared in front of me, and I caught her mother winking at me in the mirror as she went back to her other client.

"A whole week," I sighed, the strain evident in my voice.

"Hmm, and already you are changing your 'airstyle? This can only mean one thing, a man," she pouted.

"No, no man. I just, I needed a change, you know?" I didn't want to get into all the complicated reasons I had for coming here with little or no plan, but something in her eyes made it clear she understood. "Your English is so good by the way, you even have a bit of a London accent," I said.

"Oh thank you, yes I made my Erasmus in London. It is where I met my husband, Johnny," she smiled instinctively, "and now we have our little Maximilien," she said, pointing to a little baby picture peeking out from behind the mirror.

"He's so cute," I said, and I meant it, for his dark blond hair had also been styled into a quiff and he sported nothing but a nappy.

"Thank you, he's nearly three years old now," she said, shaking her head in disbelief. "My God, the time really goes so fast, non?"

I nodded in agreement, "That's why I'm a thirty-five year old single woman working in a bakery!" I laughed, suddenly seeing the absurdity of it all – trying to catch up on my twenties.

"Ah, don't tell me, you are the new replacement for Maria at the *boulangerie* on Rue De Paris?"

"Guilty."

"Well then, we are going to take very special care of you," she said, placing her hands on my shoulders.

"Why, what happened to Maria?" I asked, suddenly feeling uneasy.

"I'm not really sure, one day she was here, the next day, hop! Gone."

I gulped hard. "Hardly surprising, if she received the same warm welcome from Mme Moreau that I did".

Nicole smiled warmly. "She appears tough, but there is softness there. The years have made her that way," she explained.

I decided to reserve judgement.

"Now, the hairs, what would you like today Mademoiselle," she slipped into her hairdresser's speech and ran her fingers through my tresses, which felt divine.

"Well, I was thinking of cutting it all off actually and going for the gamine look" I announced courageously.

"Aye-aye-aye, everyone who comes to France wants this gamine, girly-girl look, *hein*? *Non*, is not for you *ma belle*," she replied.

I was taken aback by her candidness; most hairdressers at home would just go along with whatever you said and proceed to do the opposite, but they would never confront you.

"Well something drastic has to happen," I said, taking a quick sip of my coffee. Taking a leaf out of her book, I decided to say exactly what I thought, rather than being my usual overly polite self. "I want the kind of hair a man wants to play with!" As soon as I said it, I couldn't help but laugh and thankfully, so did Nicole. But there was no disagreement this time, as she walked me to the sink and set about changing my personality from the head down.

***

When I arrived back at the bakery for the afternoon shift, Mme Moreau hardly glanced my way and if she did notice my new hairstyle, she said nothing. Nicole and I had settled on a layered bob just above my collar bone with a sweeping fringe that grazed my eyelashes when it fell from behind my ears. I felt like a new person and as I passed by shop windows on my way back, I hardly recognised myself. I looked younger, more vibrant and inexplicably flirtatious. As far as I could see, I was becoming 'French'! I even ducked into a pharmacy across the street and bought fire engine red lipstick. Nicole was a breath of fresh air and to my great delight, invited me to my first '*soirée*' at a jazz club to see her husband Johnny playing bass in a gypsy jazz band. It was marvellous how, in the blink of an eye, everything had begun to change and look a lot rosier. I couldn't remember the last time anyone had invited me out on a Saturday night back home, except maybe for Aunt Gemma asking me to the pictures. Perhaps this whole idea wasn't hair-brained after all.

"*Deux chocolat chauds et deux tranches de flan Édeet, tout de suite,*" Mme Moreau croaked, waking me from my reverie. I pulled on my apron, tucked my sexy hair behind my ears and set to being the best *serveuse* in Compiègne.

Chapter 8

Saturday night finally arrived and to my blatant surprise, Mme Moreau informed me that my wages had been paid into my bank account.

"Oh good, Mr. Grumpy at the Prefecture must have received my birth cert from the Embassy," I cheered. I half expected to be told that baguettes and board were payment enough, but she stunned me further by handing me my share of the tips.

"*Pas mal*," was all she said. Not bad.

Instead of giving my usual 'people pleasing' response, 'thank you oh great one, I'm not worthy', I just agreed. "*Je sais* – I know". I thought I saw the trace of a smile, but it was probably a trick of the light, for she had already switched off the main lights, leaving us in relative darkness.

"*À lundi*," she said, bidding me farewell until Monday.

I was looking forward to having Sunday all to myself and not having to get up with the birds. Although this made me recall the noises that had woken me up every night since my arrival and feeling bold, I decided to ask her about them.

"Madame Moreau, do you know what all the banging is at night? I keep hearing noises in the building."

That familiar veil of irritation came over her face as she grunted, "*Ce bâtiment est très vieux Mademoiselle*, all old buildings make noise – zey 'ave to breath, non?"

"That's what I thought, all the old timbers and everything. Unless you're getting up each night and dancing Riverdance on the stairs!" I said this extremely quickly in a thick Dublin accent, still she pretended to understand and gave a withering nod before mounting the stairs to her apartment. "Charming, as ever Mme Moreau, pleasure working with you," I scoffed in her absence. This kind of encounter would have really upset me back home, but here, I was getting used to the whole 'say what you feel' culture. It wasn't anything personal, just a means of expression unburdened by the kind of social etiquette that prevents Irish people from saying what they mean.

Back in my own little room, which I was really growing quite fond of, I indulged in my preparations for the night ahead. I turned on the old fashioned radio high on the shelf above the stove and found a station playing all American jazz. It was like the old days at home with my mother; Ella Fitzgerald, Louis Armstrong and Old Blue Eyes serenaded me as I showered and pulled on my trusty little black dress. I longed for Nicole's curves, but realised I would soon have my own if I kept wolfing down the bakery's products. Like a true *française*, I enjoyed a fresh baguette with my evening meal and even took to eating a croissant every morning for breakfast. While my breasts were more like peaches compared to Nicole's melons, they still looked quite perky and with my new hairdo exposing my neckline, I felt confident enough to go without wearing a scarf over the rather daring neckline. Well, that said, it was hardly plunging, but it was taking a shallow dive in that direction.

Trotting through the cobbled streets in a pair of kitten heel shoes, I almost lost my balance once or twice as a sparkling night frost set in. Following the directions Nicole had given me, I made my way to the club through the winding streets of the old *quartier*. From the outside, it looked very unassuming with blue velvet drapes covering the windows and those plastic coloured beads that scream student flat, forming a curtain at the front door. The name overhead, written in blue tube lighting, read 'Nostalgie', which sounded close enough to the name Nicole had given me. Although I

tried to act like meeting friends in a bar in France on a
Saturday night was just routine, secretly my stomach tingled
with nerves. As soon as I walked through the door however, I
saw Nicole's face keeping an eye out for me, and her genuine
smile on seeing me made me relax.

"Hey Eddie!" she cried and embraced me with a kiss on
each cheek. "You look *ravissante*!" she beamed.

She looked ravishing herself, in a red strapless dress with
black pearls.

"This place is..." I trailed off.

"*Petit*?" She finished my sentence. "I know, it's not much to
look at, but it's the only jazz bar in town and Johnny's band
has their residency here."

Looking around, I could see why the regulars stayed loyal to
the place. It was unpretentious and unique, with its abstract
paintings and burgundy coloured walls. The tables were
huddled closely together for a cosy feel and lit by little
candles in wine bottles. The waiter was covered in tattoos and
sported a gravity-defying quiff. It felt good to be among a
crowd who weren't afraid to express themselves. Nostalgie
was the kind of place that celebrated individuality and
difference, acceptance was guaranteed. It was like all those
years spent at home watching movies and listening to music
from another time, had always made me feel out of step with
my peers and the rest of the world. It was all social media, X
factor and other kinds of pop culture that made me want to
retreat further into the world my mother and I had created.
But in this place, with these people, I finally felt like I had
found my place in the world and it felt blissful.

Nicole ordered the drinks and without hesitation, I found
myself sipping on a Mai Tai, which tasted like the nectar of
the Gods. The dark rum warmed my throat after my chilly

walk and loosened the tight grip of wariness that had held me captive for such a long time.

"Eddie, I want to introduce you to my sister Cathy and her girlfriend Cécile," said Nicole, leaning back so we could all go through the kissing hello process again. "This is my Irish friend Édith."

A chorus of '*Bonsoirs*' followed and while I didn't think anything of it at first, I began to notice that the two girls were constantly holding hands and caressing. I struggled desperately to be cool about it, which probably achieved the opposite effect.

"It's okay," Nicole whispered, noticing my clumsiness, "it was awkward for me too at first, but then you realise, it's just love so, it doesn't matter, you know?"

I just smiled and, not for the first time, wished I could be less self-conscious like Nicole.

"Now tell me, how is life at La Boulangerie?"

"Oh you know, Madame Moreau simply can't do enough for me, like even today, she gave me a bonus in my salary for being the employee of the month."

Nicole held her head to one side in a confused look.

"I'm being sarcastic; she still ignores me for the most part and grunts at me when she has to. It's working out fantastically well."

Nicole laughed a deep throaty laugh. "You are a funny one!"

"Well I'm glad my French adventure is amusing someone," I sighed.

I'm not ashamed to say that at that point, I was glowing with the satisfaction of belonging. It had been so long since I'd connected with anyone or had a conversation with someone who didn't know all the heartache of the past year and a half. I could laugh and joke and just be Edith again.

"Manu is a sweet kid, even though he never has much to say for himself," I continued.

"Manu is a smart one, you know, he will take over the bakery after Mme Moreau…" Nicole trailed off delicately.

"Are they related or something?" I asked, unable to imagine why a bright young teenager would want to spend his days working with a cranky old dinosaur.

"I'm not certain, but he has been at the bakery since he was a child. It's so long now that I cannot remember. But I know he wishes to, how do you say, make an apprentice to become a master baker. Perhaps he will be the next Monsieur Moreau."

Monsieur Moreau? This was news to me. "Mme Moreau's married?" I gasped.

"No, no, it was her father or her uncle I think. He's dead for some time now."

"Oh," I felt a pang of sympathy for her. "So I wonder who the master baker is now then? I've never met him and she's hardly mentioned it – except to say that I am not to enter the basement on pain of death."

"I will ask my mother, if you like. She grew up in the neighbourhood, so I'm sure she will remember."

Just then, a group of musicians took to the stage and began warming up their instruments.

"Look, is my husband Johnny on stage," she waved at a tall, muscular man with dark blonde hair swept to one side, revealing a close shave on the other. He was sporting the suspenders look, with long black baggy trousers. He spun his bass around as the band leader introduced the musicians – Johnny on bass, Frankie on the snare drum, Laurent on violin and himself, Stéphane on guitar. Both he and the violinist sported skinny moustaches, while the drummer displayed magnificent sideburns and a ponytail of jet black hair. They were a raggle-taggle group of musicians if ever I saw one, but when they started to play, it all made sense. Nicole stood and cheered loudly as they broke into an up-tempo number I didn't recognise, that just oozed cool. I sipped happily on my cocktail as I watched my feet take on a life of their own to the rhythm.

"You like?" Nicole yelled over the crowd.

"I love!"

I was living all of my fantasies and had the unusual feeling of completeness. I glanced around the bar at my fellow patrons, chatting animatedly and carrying off the style of the 40's and 50's with aplomb. It was then that I noticed a solitary figure emerging from a physical argument with the beaded curtains and taking the first available seat at the bar. He was in a dark grey suit with a black tie loosened at his neck and had a look of someone far too serious to enjoy jazz. Then again, I reasoned, that was probably how I looked when I was alone and uncomfortable. From my vantage point, I could clearly see him, while I remained hidden behind a conveniently placed palm tree. I studied his face unabashedly and while it was clear that he did not have the obvious good looks of some of the other men I had spotted around the club, I realised that I couldn't stop staring. His hair was neither long nor entirely short either and it had a slight wave that gave him a boyish look. His eyebrows were knitted together in a stern look and his high cheekbones only exaggerated his slender physique. However, when the barman brought him his drink and he smiled a thank you, his dazzling blue eyes almost pierced my heart from across the room. As if that wasn't enough, his lips transformed into the most endearing smile, as the corners turned down slightly, creating little dimples in his cheeks.

At this stage Nicole elbowed my arm and asked what I was looking at.

"What me? Oh nothing really, just enjoying the place."

"*N'importe quoi* – or should I say whatever *ma belle*, you've spotted someone. Like a lioness and her prey. *Allez*, tell me who it is," she insisted.

This was the most fun I'd had in years and it made me feel like a schoolgirl again, pointing out the guy I liked. All I needed to do now was ask her to go and tell him that her friend fancied him.

"Ahh, yes I see, *il est mignon non*? He's cute. Why don't you go over and talk to him," she suggested, just like that.

"Are you kidding? I've never approached a guy. I'm, you know, old school." She may as well have asked me to take all my clothes off then and there. It was unthinkable.

Nicole rolled her eyes in that impatient manner she had with dilly-dalliers. "Okay Mademoiselle 'Old School', why don't you walk by on your way to the toilet and give him the look," she replied.

"The look?"

"The look, you know, the look that says 'come and get me'," she laughed, jiggling her boobs and pouting her lips.

I thought about it for a second; I mean here I was, starting a new life and things were actually beginning to fall into place for me. I felt good about myself, my hair was sexy, my red lipstick on, what did I have to lose? Plus, at the age of thirty-five, was it really realistic to sit around and wait for the man to come to me?

"Right, I'll do it!" I announced, knocking back the rest of my cocktail, which unfortunately went down the wrong way, inducing a temporary coughing fit.

"*Allez*, come on, you're fine," Nicole soothed, giving me a napkin. "Just walk over there and be hot!"

"Will do!"

I shimmied my way through the maze of tables, as though shimmying was my modus operandi. As I was about to pass by the bar, my target's features had returned to that of a brooding grizzly bear, so I aborted the entire operation and took a swinging right turn towards the gents toilets. Backtracking along the blue velvet drapes at the rear of the club, I managed to eke my way along to the ladies and dived into a cubicle. My heart was racing, as though I had just cheated death, but instead of feeling like an idiot (as I usually did in those situations) I just laughed out loud to myself. Looking back over the whole thing, I realised how funny it was that his stern look had put me off 'being hot' as Nicole had ordered.

'Oh well, maybe next time', I reassured myself, as I turned around to get some tissue paper. With horror, I realised I was in some kind of shower cubicle, only, there was no shower. My eyes travelled up and down, from the ceramic 'shower tray' for want of a better word at the base, to the cistern complete with pull chain, high over my head. I couldn't work it out. Where was the toilet seat? There was basically a hole in the ground and two 'feet shaped' pads to the front. As I turned backwards to place my feet on the raised pads, purely in an effort to see if this was what the constructors had in mind, it became nauseatingly clear that this was the toilet and patrons were obviously expected to hover over the hole and hope for the best. I stood back in revulsion, vowing that no matter what the culture, I was going to keep my dignity. I stormed out and pushed back the door of the second cubicle, only to discover an identical set up. I shook my head in disbelief and decided that if nature called, I would gladly find the nearest McDonalds and take my, um, business there.

Still in a state of lavatory shock, I walked back into the club which at this stage was really humming with smooth jazz and hard liquor. I gave a sideways glance to the bar and to my disappointment, I noticed that old blue eyes had left his seat. I knew it shouldn't really matter, I mean I didn't even know the guy and the chances of him already having hitched his wagon to another were disappointingly high. But I felt my heart sink a little at the loss of getting to find out. People had taken to dancing wherever they happened to be and I almost ended up in something of a threesome in an effort to get past a couple lost in a slow dance. So I didn't even notice when I returned to my seat that Nicole was now chatting animatedly to a man in a grey suit. My heart actually stopped for a second, as did everything else in the room, when he looked up into my face and gave me an ever-so-cool nod of recognition.

"Ah Édith, I would like you to meet Hugo Chadwick, Hugo this is my friend Édith from Ireland" Nicole did the honours without the faintest trace of guile in her wide, innocent eyes.

I instinctively went to shake his hands, forgetting all about the obligatory kiss, whereas he stood to embrace me appropriately or '*faire la bise*'. This miscommunication meant that I had embarrassingly greeted his groin while he lightly kissed me on my temple as I bent forward.

"*Enchanté*," he said, kindly over-looking my faux-pas. I couldn't remember anyone in my life ever having been genuinely enchanted to meet me. His deep, sultry voice reverberated in my ears and I wasn't at all sure my heart could take it as it made its reservations known with a loud thumping in double quick time. As we all sat around the table again, an awkward silence descended.

"Hugo has just arrived from London," Nicole spoke to me as though speaking to a child unwilling to take advantage of the opportunity dropped neatly in her lap. Her widening stare provoked me into action and I grabbed the lifeline with both hands.

"Oh, you're not French then? I thought with a name like Hugo…" I trailed off, aware that my voice sounded remarkably nothing like me.

"Half and half I'm afraid, my mother is French and my father is English," he replied, still with that serious look that made it difficult to decipher whether or not he liked you or was simply tolerating you.

"*C'est comme Johnny et moi!*" Nicole interrupted, then thought better of getting stuck between the two of us again and excused herself to move closer to the stage.

I have no shame in admitting, I was nervous as hell. Here was this attractive, intelligent, cosmopolitan guy and I couldn't think of the first thing to say. Do you come here often swam around my head a few times before I formed a less cliché question. "What brings you to Compiègne?" Well done Edie, I thought, that almost sounded like something a normal person would say.

"Oh this and that," he said with a non-committal shrug, but to my delight, he moved to Nicole's chair to sit closer to me. I took a large gulp of my Mai Tai.

"Do you like jazz?" he countered.

"Do I like jazz?" I smiled and felt something playful inside me prompt the reply, "Honey, I love jazz!"

Chapter 9

Something weird happened and the only way I can explain it is to blame the Mai Tais. Nicole's husband's band played 'Let's Fall In Love' and the thought of birds, bees and everything else on the planet doing it, made it so completely unnatural not to. Hugo asked me to dance and that was when my fate was sealed. Had we sat chatting at the table, we may well have gone our separate ways that night. But once I fell into his embrace, I think we both knew where the evening would lead.

He didn't strike me as someone who would make a good dancer, with his professional veneer and English reserve giving him a stymied air. But when we started to move on the dance floor, his French genes must have taken over, for he moved me in a practised manner with ease and confidence. We didn't speak very much, but I felt so connected to him on a physical level, that my inhibitions around him vanished. When the band finally wrapped up with a version of Benny Goodman's hectic "Sing, Sing, Sing," we admitted defeat and returned to the table where Hugo ordered another round of drinks.

"Can all Irish women dance as well as you?" he asked, handing me what I assumed to be a Martini.

"Of course, but we don't like to brag about it, you know," I said. Taking a sip of my drink, I looked up to find myself the subject of the most intense stare. "What is it?" I asked, checking to see if my hair was okay or whether one of my boobs had fallen out.

"Nothing," he said, looking away and self-consciously rubbing the back of his neck. "Or everything, actually".

"What?" I said again, but just then Nicole, her sisters and her husband Johnny arrived back to the table. She made all of the introductions once again and I was pleased to see her with her arms wrapped around her husband's waist. It was clear they were mad about each other, as he caressed her neck and placed kisses on her cheek at every break in conversation. A soundtrack of cool jazz played over the sound system replacing the live musicians, and the tempo slowed to a soft sway. I was surrounded by love, jazz and *je ne sais quoi* and it was intoxicating. We all chatted easily as if we had known each other forever and as Chet Baker crooned, "I fall in love too easily" I felt like I was starring in my own Hollywood romance. When it came time to leave, I gave Nicole the universal girly wink that said 'come to the toilets for a chat'.

"What do you think?" I said, realising that I was looking for guidance from a girl I had only just met, about a guy we hardly knew.

"Go for it!" she enthused, putting on her bright berry lipstick. "Why not?"

"Eh, because he could be an axe murderer?" I pointed out.

"Édith," she said, gripping both my shoulders, "you have my mobile if you need me and if it doesn't feel right to you, just leave. But listen ma belle, you came to France to change your ideas a bit, *non*? So follow your heart this time, it is okay to have some fun sometimes you know!"

"You're right, you're right. I'm just not used to being this person, you know? I've always tried to be so careful, but tonight, I just feel like taking a holiday from myself and all of my stupid rules." I could tell she understood and we embraced like life-long friends. "But just tell me one more thing, are these really toilets?"

***

"So Edith, you haven't told me what brought you to Compiègne," Hugo asked, as we walked along the riverbank. The heightened sense of enjoyment I got out of hearing him say my name made me feel like a complete nerd, but his accent was so delicious I couldn't help it.

"Oh definitely the Turkish toilets," I joked, sounding decidedly less posh than Hugo's tutored English accent. The cool night air came as a shock after the hot and sweaty atmosphere of Nostalgie, yet I somehow felt buffeted against the cold when Hugo offered his arm in such a chivalrous move that made my heart glow a little brighter. "Seriously though, have you seen those things? I mean what century is this?" I asked, starting to wish I hadn't brought it up.

"Well, aside from French plumbing, what brings an Irish girl to a town like this?"

"I'm a singer," I had blurted it out before my brain had time to restrain me. I had no idea where the fabrication came from; all I knew was that I wanted to sound a little more interesting than a mid-life crisis victim working in a shop.

"Really?" he asked, genuinely impressed by my not so run of the mill answer. In fact, he seemed so impressed that I was reluctant to correct him. Besides, what harm would it do to tell a little white lie? As Nicole said, I wasn't marrying the guy.

"Yes, well I mean, I'm working in a bakery here until I get my big break, but yes, I'm a singer."

"What genre of music do you sing? Do you write your own songs?" he enthused, unaware of the pressure he was putting on me to make up the answers.

"Mainly jazz," I said, trying to keep it vague and nonchalant.

"Ah, thus Nostalgie," he concluded.

56

"Mhmm, and what about you? You never said what it was you do?" I deflected, buying myself some time from my own ridiculously tall tale.

"Um, well I do some photography," he said.

"Really, oh that sounds so interesting! What area do you work in, commercial, editorial, fashion?"

"Bit of everything really, I'm not very good at it though."

I felt sure this statement of self-deprecation was just a gentlemanly way of not blowing his own trumpet.

"In fact I'm off to Toulouse in the morning to, eh, take some shots on location," he added

"Toulouse – that's in the south right?" I was impressed, what an interesting life, travelling around taking artsy shots on location. I thought of all those black and white images I used to line my wall with as a teenager with couples kissing in front of famous places like the Eiffel Tower.

"Yes, my mother lives there, so it's sort of a working holiday really."

We came to a bench that offered a beautiful view of the Pont Solférino bridge, with its lights reflected in the flowing waters of the River Oise. Despite the chill, the late hour and the absurdity of it, we both instinctively sat down in order to prolong the evening.

"You're not really like anyone I've ever met before," he said.

"I hope you mean that in a good way," I replied, still unable to read him.

"I think it's good," he grinned in that way that made my stomach flip. "I thought Irish women were more…" he cut off here on seeing my face.

"More what?" I challenged defensively.

"Oh I don't know, uncouth?" he said, guarding himself with his hands in front of his face.

"What?" I knew by his manner that he was play-acting, but I couldn't let this slight go unpunished. "Well that's interesting because I thought English people were stuck up, snotty prigs and guess what? I was right!" I punched him hard in the arm.

"Okay, I'm sorry, I'm sorry," he said "I merely meant that Irish women can be quite, you know, fiery? I humbly ask your forgiveness," he bowed theatrically.

"I don't know, I'll think about it Mr. Chadwick but I can't promise anything." I folded my arms and turned towards the river, all too aware that it was his intention to provoke me and as every girl knows, a guy who insults you clearly fancies the pants off you. But did that still apply when you were closer to 40 than 14?

"I can be fiery," I mumbled, but I hardly had time to consider my next comeback, for before I knew it, he had reached his hand over to my cheek and turned my face to meet his waiting lips. He kissed me softly and deeply; the warmth of his breath on my skin intoxicating. We stayed there, kissing each other compulsively for what seemed like hours.

When I finally broke free, I felt light-headed and not altogether aware of my surroundings. It was the most beautiful feeling of complete abandonment, that I did not want it to end. He must have felt the same, as he held my hand in his while we talked of everything and nothing.

"Do you make a habit of kissing uncouth Irish women on park benches Mr. Chadwick?"

"No," he replied, with those furrowed eyebrows creating a mock look of sincerity, "I try not to, but one has to make the odd exception for extremely attractive Irish women," he replied. "In fact, I have a very strict rule about kissing women on benches after midnight," he continued.

"Oh, and what is that then?" I couldn't help but hang on his every word.

58

"Well, you see the thing is, they have to sing me a song."

Oh dear. I had well and truly landed myself in it. When he asked me what I was doing in France, I felt compelled to embellish the truth and for some reason, a long-forgotten dream I had had about being a singer just popped into my head. I used to sing for my mother all the time – all the old standards – but I had never done anything about it. It was as if I had become possessed by my younger self, who was intent on living out all of the dreams I had never been able to fulfil.

"I really couldn't," I began nervously.

"I know, the crowd must be putting you off," he moved his wrist to take in the family of ducks sailing obliviously past us on the river's gentle current.

"Oh shut up Hugo, I just can't, I'd be embarrassed. There's no music for starters," I complained, knowing this was going to be a losing battle as he had begun to kiss my neck, all the while whispering gentle encouragements. I'm not sure if it was the drink, the magic of the star-speckled night, or if it was just him, but I started to think, what did it matter? I'd probably never see him again, so why not live out this little fantasy until the dawn arrived and broke the spell? Taking a deep breath and a giant leap of faith, I closed my eyes and sang my old favourite, 'Dream A Little Dream Of Me'. I hadn't sung in so long, I knew I was a little rusty, but there was something in the tone of my voice that even surprised me. It was richer, deeper and more emotive than ever before.

"That was beautiful Edith, thank you," Hugo said, still holding my hand and looking at me with that intense stare that made me feel like I had no place to hide from him.

"The last time I sang that song was for my mother," I told him. "She's… she's passed now."

He said nothing, but took me into his arms. I didn't cry, but I just let myself be held and it felt like such a relief. I hadn't told anyone here the real reason behind my sudden decision to come to France, and even though this was probably the most inopportune moment to open up, not to mention the wrong person, it just happened.

"My father," he said simply, still holding me in his arms. "It's about fifteen years ago now, I was 24. You just grow accustomed to their absence I suppose. I mean, we didn't even get on, but still it changes everything."

His honesty endeared him to me and he was right. It did change everything; so much so that I had to change who I was in order to feel some kind of control over my life again.

"He probably would have warned me off someone like you," he smiled.

"Eh, what do you mean by that?" I asked, rousing myself.

"Easy old girl, I'm actually paying you a compliment. You're a free spirit, courageous and, well you're fun. The antithesis of the kind of woman he would have wanted me to settle down with."

"What, you mean restricted, weak and dull?"

"Bingo," he said, looking out across the water.

That stare concealed so much that I wanted to know, but the cold had finally broken through to my skin and I was desperate for a warm drink.

"Do you want to come back to mine for coffee?"

"Is that a euphemism or actual coffee, because I'd murder a coffee," he said sarcastically.

This garnered him another punch in the arm.

"I'm being assaulted here, you know. Oi, gendarmes, arrest this woman!" he shouted at some students passing over the bridge who responded with all sorts of taunts and gestures that happily, I did not understand.

The walk took far longer than necessary, because with every few strides, we were both drawn to each other's lips. My arms reached under his overcoat and embraced the warmth of his body as we kissed by the Crêperie, the Tabac, and eventually reached the boulangerie.

"So, this is me," I said, just like they do in the movies. "But Mme Moreau, my boss that is, lives in the apartment below me so you'll have to be quiet…" I could see his features changing completely so I asked what was the matter.

"You work here, for Mme Moreau?"

"Yes, why do you know her? She's not exactly boss of the year material, but I'm really growing to like the place and the accommodation is free so …" I smiled, but his expression remained unchanged.

"You know, I'd best be getting back, I've got that early TGV to Toulouse in the morning and I don't want to cause any trouble with your boss," he explained.

"Oh." I failed miserably to keep the tone of disappointment from my voice, so decided to make up for it by babbling on endlessly about Mme Moreau. "Of course, you're right, it's only my first week here and she might start to question my morals along with everything else if I bring a guy home on my first weekend."

He smiled and held my hand, as if in two minds whether to tell me something. I decided to act like the free spirited, courageous and fun person he thought me to be.

"I've had a wonderful evening Mr. Chadwick," I said, as I kissed him lightly on both cheeks "and it was lovely to meet you."

"The pleasure has been entirely mine, Miss Lane," he responded, lifting both of my hands and kissing each of them tenderly. "I hope to see you again," he added, lifting those piercing blue eyes.

"Well, if you ever need a baguette, you know where I am," I smiled.

He pulled me close then and gave me a ravishingly good kiss on the lips, leaving me slightly tipsy.

"Goodnight Edith," he said, as he turned to leave.

"Goodnight Hugo."

I climbed the creaky old stairs to my apartment, still in a daze. I hung my coat up by the door and slipped out of my shoes, smiling inanely all the while. No sooner had I turned on the lamp by the window looking out onto the street when I heard stones ricocheting off the glass. I skipped to the window and looked down at Hugo about to take another aim.

"Oi, what are you doing, you'll wake the dragon!" I hissed.

"Ah, what light from yonder window breaks," he called amusingly.

"Quit goofing around or you'll get me the sack Romeo," I said, unable to conceal my pleasure at seeing him standing down there, acting like a romantic fool, for me.

"I just wanted to let you know, I'll be out of town for a while, but I'd like to take you out to dinner when I get back."

"That would be lovely," I whispered down to him.

"It's a date then," he confirmed.

"Yes, it's a date" I echoed, almost in confirmation to myself. I couldn't really believe this was happening.

"*Bonne nuit* Edith."

I waved silently and blew him a kiss, which he caught and held to his heart, then half collapsed as if I had shot him. All too soon, he turned to go and I could have sworn I heard him whistling the tune 'Dream a Little Dream of Me', but I couldn't have been sure.

Chapter 10

My mother had been ill for a long time. She had known from birth that her time would be limited once she was diagnosed with Cystic Fibrosis (or 65 Roses as I used to call it when I was a child). But it was not a life-sentence that damned her - quite the opposite in fact. She was determined to live life to the full and make the most of every experience. She had to spend a lot of time in hospital, dealing with infections and other complications, so we had to try our best to make it fun. She and my father were what you would call high school sweethearts. She always said she knew he was the one when, after she told him about her illness, he told her they'd just have to hurry up and live a life's worth of memories in half the time.

"Telling someone you have an incurable disease is a sure-fire way of separating the men from the boys," she often told me.

That's why they decided to have me when my mother was only 18. My father was 20 at the time and got a job as the desserts chef in a top cafe in Dublin, where I ended up waitressing years later. He packed it all in when she began to get really sick and took on work as a taxi driver, which still meant long hours, but at least he could work the shifts that suited him. The average life expectancy for Cystic Fibrosis sufferers is 40, so we cherished every year we shared beyond that. They both made it quite clear that I didn't need to stay at home. 'I can get home help', my father would always insist. But I was their only child. It had always been the three of us against the world and it just didn't feel right to abandon them when they needed me the most. Working alongside my father's colleagues at the cafe was like being part of an extended family, so I felt at home there. I converted the garage at home into a little studio apartment with Dad's help, so I had my own front door while still living at home. We managed quite well between us and despite their protestations; I knew my parents were glad to have me close by.

With the hindsight that only time can give, I realised too late why they wanted me to make a life for myself. There are some things that are better done when you're young and foolhardy and unafraid of failure. That's the time when you build your career, meet your future husband, carve out your own space in the world. But I couldn't do it and never once regretted the time I spent laughing, crying, watching old movies or sharing a box of chocolates with my mother. She stayed at home a lot to prevent any risk of infection, so we turned it into our own little world indoors. I avoided the big bad world for so long, but now I would have to turn the natural order of things on its head. At the age of 35 and something of a late bloomer, I was determined to live my student years.

I awoke to church bells ringing and for the first time since I had arrived, I realised I had slept the night through. Picking up my phone, I saw the time was 9.30 and despite a medium-sized hangover, I felt well-rested. My thoughts instantly turned to Hugo and I couldn't help the smile that kept creeping across my face when I replayed our evening together. When I eventually got around to taking a shower, I absent-mindedly began humming to myself and to my complete embarrassment, remembered singing for him.

"Oh my God!" I screeched, putting my hands to my mouth, while the water cascaded down my back. I shoved my head underneath the temperamental spout that changed force on a whim. Still, I couldn't help but laugh, because the entire night had been so surreal. Even telling him about my mother only seemed to forge a stronger bond. 'Hugo' I whispered, just wanting to say his name.

My last boyfriend was a postman. My mother always joked that the only way I would ever meet a man was if he came to our house and knocked on the door, and strangely enough that is exactly what happened. He was kind and always did his best to make me laugh. When he asked me out, I didn't really feel butterflies, but rather a practical resignation to it all. I knew the chances of me meeting someone were slim, so I thought I'd better make the best of this one chance. I ignored it for as long as possible, because I really did want to love him and marry and maybe even start a family. It would have been… well it would have been practical. But I came to the realisation that I could be practical all on my own and I didn't have to drag someone into a loveless relationship to achieve it. I knew he was disappointed. Even my Dad seemed upset. But my mother just smiled and patted my hand.

"You'll know when it's right," was all she said.

Wrapped in a towel, I tip-toed across the floorboards to where my phone lay flashing on the bed. A text from Nicole inviting me to Sunday lunch at her mother's house. She couldn't have picked a better time to reach out the hand of friendship, for all these thoughts of home were making me pine for some familial company. I heard Mme Moreau returning home, most likely from Sunday mass. I wondered if she was lonely and whether she had any invites to Sunday lunch. I pushed the thought from my head. I would be soon enough seeing her in the morning.

Wearing my most comfortable pair of skinny jeans, furry boots and knitted cardigan with a colourful scarf, I set off to find Nicole's family home. It wasn't far from the centre and despite the maze-like nature of the town, I found it easily enough. On Rue Sainte Antoine the detached houses all seemed to have their own unique character and design. Nicole's mother's house had a curved roof that made room for one little window at the top of the house and then gradually stretched out to incorporate more windows on the first floor. An iron gate opened onto a gravel drive with shrubs lining the way up to the steps at the front door which was painted a verdant green, with coloured glass panels on each side.

"Bonjour, bonjour," Mme Dubois hugged and kissed me like a long-lost friend and insisted that I call her Jacqueline. Looking every inch the glamour puss in a leopard skin blouse and matching skirt, she invited me in and took my coat and bag and hung them in a cupboard under the stairs, only to discover a little monster waiting inside who almost knocked her over with fright.

"*Maxi, mais qu'est ce que tu fous là-dedans?*" she admonished him lightly, wagging her finger and making lots of gestures he happily ignored. Nicole's little boy ran across the parquet floor, straight towards me and then stopped just as fast. He pulled a toy gun out of his pocket, carefully took aim and shot me in the stomach. I couldn't see anything for it but to play along, so I folded in two with pain etched across my face. His laughter rang through the house and offering me a hand back up, I knew I had passed the test.

"Max, try not to shoot our friends please," his mother begged, coming out of the kitchen. Nicole embraced me warmly and brought me down into the kitchen, which took up the entire back of the house, with windows onto the garden at the rear. A giant table with countless chairs sat in the centre of the room, while an old range heated pots and pans in the corner. It was vintage yet chic, old fashioned but timeless. Johnny appeared rather incongruously from the garden, with a handful of rosemary.

66

"Alright Edith? Good to see you again," he said, kissing me. It felt weird doing '*la bise*' with an Englishman, but as they say, when in Rome, or Compiègne in my case. "How's the head?" he jeered, but Nicole elbowed him into silence.

We ate a hearty meal of roast chicken with lemon and rosemary and lots of roast garlic potatoes on the side. I brought the dessert, which was a raspberry tart with crème anglaise. I passed on the wine, insisting that I would need a clear head to be up at six the next morning. I knew Nicole was desperate to ask me about Hugo, but as she sensed I wasn't keen to discuss in front of everyone, we talked about the bakery instead.

"*Mme Moreau? Je la connais depuis des années,*" Jacqueline began. Nicole translated in case there were any parts I didn't understand.

"Mister Moreau, Geneviève's father died in the late sixties and she's been running the place herself since then," Nicole explained, bobbing Max on her knee as he recreated a war scene with some soldiers and leftover raspberries on the table. "She must be at least eighty years old."

"Bloody hell! Eighty? But she struts around that shop like a spring chicken!" I gasped, waiting for Nicole to translate. Finding out her Christian name was also something of a shock. The name Geneviève was somehow too sweet for the tough woman who greeted me with a scowl every morning.

"She's had a hard life, according to Mum. Her mother remembers the Regime having several run-ins with Monsieur Moreau during the war."

This was such an eye-opener for me. All I had seen was a grumpy old woman, with little or no time for pleasantries. This was creating an entirely new picture of a young girl that had lived through the war with her father, withstood the tyranny of German occupation and still managed to keep his legacy alive.

"So, who has taken over the baking since Monsieur Moreau's death?" I asked. "The basement is strictly off limits for me," I added, still stung by her lack of trust in me.

"*Je ne sais pas*," Jacqueline admitted.

"It's strange because I've been there for two weeks now and I never see anyone going in or coming out. And unless they're milling their own flour underground, I don't know how they're getting it in, because no deliveries show up either."

Johnny brought a large pot of coffee to the table along with a glass jar of biscotti. Even though I felt fit to burst, I couldn't resist the almond scented biscuits.

"Sounds like you've got a bit of a mystery on your hands," Johnny said. "The haunted bakery, where no one is seen going in and no one is seen going out, woooooo!" he began to laugh, while Max imitated his not-so-scary ghost impression.

"I'm serious," I persisted, "Mme Moreau has all the bread stocked up and Manu has loaded his deliveries before I even get up. There's never any sign of the baker. I just assumed they take up the bread themselves from the kitchen, but why not let me go down? I mean, I'm supposed to be taking over as manager for God's sake."

"Manager?" Jacqueline repeated in a cute French accent.

"Well that was the job title. I think she's going to have to retire soon. Even if she finds it difficult to let go of the reins, her arthritis won't let her carry on without help for much longer."

"Maman says she must like you – the last girl Maria only lasted two days."

I knew this was meant to comfort me, but somehow it didn't.

"I know, we'll all start keeping a closer eye on the bakery and see if we can't catch them out. Maybe they're laundering money down there or cooking up some Class A drugs!" joked Johnny.

"You'll have to eat your words when I discover some, I don't know, secret dough society or something," I said, playing along.

As the dark evening sky settled in around the house, I made the reluctant move to go home.

"*Merci pour tout*," I said to Jacqueline, kissing her warmly at the door.

"*Je t'en prie chérie*," she said, as if it was nothing.

Max was asleep on a little settee near the fire and Nicole didn't want to wake him just yet for their walk home. They lived in an apartment near the university, which was convenient to her mother's house and the salon.

"I will walk Edith to the end of the road while you wash the dishes Johnny, *d'accord*?" she smiled at him sweetly.

"You see what I have to put up with Edith?" he said, kissing me goodbye. "They treat me like their English slave; cooking, cleaning and I won't say what else to save your blushes!"

Nicole threw a tea towel at his head to quieten him, but it didn't work.

"We'll see you at Nostalgie next week, yeah?" he shouted after me.

"Oh yeah, I'd love to. Your band was amazing, I really enjoyed it," I said sincerely. "But who's that Django Reinhardt you kept talking about? Was that his music you were playing?"

"Oh my God, you're joking right?" he asked in all seriousness. "Django Reinhardt; you don't know who he is?" he asked.

On seeing my newly acquired Gallic shrug, he begged us to wait for five minutes while he dug into his rucksack and produced a CD.

"Django Reinhardt is only the king of gypsy jazz," he informed me, barely excusing my philistine ignorance. "You've got to take this home," he said "listen to it, familiarise yourself with it and we'll pretend this conversation never happened, right?"

"Right!" I promised.

A drizzle had begun, so I told Nicole she needn't bother stepping outside.

"But I wanted to hear all about Hugo!" she said.

"I know, but nothing happened. Well, nothing and everything," I admitted hopelessly.

"Okay, tomorrow, meet me after work for a glass and tell me everything, yes?"

"Alright, everything, I promise."

Chapter 11

On Monday morning I awoke at my usual time of 6:00 am.
I pulled the shutters and gaped out the window at every
opportunity, looking out onto the street for any clandestine
behaviour that might betray the Moreau's, with a toothbrush
in my mouth or a hairbrush tangled in my hair. The street was
quiet, nothing stirred. I skipped breakfast and tumbled
downstairs for 6.30, but Mme Moreau, who had seemingly
risen at some unthinkable hour, was already unloading baskets
of freshly made bread on to the shelves. Manu was yet to
arrive, but the boxes awaiting delivery were already neatly
stacked by the door. How did she do it all? And at her age?

"*Bonjour Mme Moreau*," I said, startling her.

"*Bonjour Édith*," she replied.

I thought she looked a little tired this morning and so I
offered to make her a coffee before we opened. This really
took her by surprise and even though she turned me down, I
felt something alter between us. I quietly went about my
work, and opened the door for Manu when he arrived. The
rain was pouring down and I really felt for him, having to get
on that scooter and deliver bread. He wrapped a small
tarpaulin over the boxes and zoomed off without much ado.

"He's a good lad, isn't he?" I said to Mme Moreau. "*Il est
bien*," I repeated.

"*Il travaille bien, oui*" she agreed, giving very little away.

"*Il habite près d'ici?*" I pressed on, trying to find out if he
lived in the area or who his family were and perhaps, how he
ended up working here.

"En haut," she lifted her head briefly, signalling above our
heads.

"He lives with you?" I said, unable to hide my incredulity. Thanks to that little faut-pas, I was back to receiving grunts and hand signals that I should get on with my work. And with that the first few customers of the morning came in and there was no further time to think about it.

Working with freshly baked goods all day brought back so many of the wonderful childhood memories that I had stored away for a long time. When my father gave up his position as pastry chef, he turned our kitchen at home into a playground for his artistic expression. My mother and I were often treated to light and airy profiteroles, oozing with cream and smothered in chocolate, or dark chocolate tortes with roasted hazelnut crusts. My favourite were the cakes and at his side, I became quite proficient myself and made a mean spicy carrot cake. He would always say that you could tell a lot about a baker by his choice of ingredients. Needless to say, I was intrigued to meet the master baker who kick-started my appetite with his delicious breads and sinfully good pastries. Yet, he remained shrouded in mystery, hidden in the Moreaus' basement.

In an effort to become better acquainted with his produce at least, I spent my lunch time doing a little taste test in the café. I told Mme Moreau that I wished to become more familiar with the different kinds of bread and she just shrugged indifference. Having the place to myself, I brought my little portable stereo downstairs and put on Johnny's CD of Django Reinhardt. As soon as the jazzy guitar began to play, I instantly fell in love with gypsy jazz and found myself swaying along to the rhythm as I began picking out which breads to try. Leaving aside the well-known baguettes and traditional *pain de campagne* and *pain complet* (white and brown) I gathered the more unusual looking breads into my arms and found myself salivating with the scent of fresh, crusty bread. So I sat down at a little table by the window and using a cutting board and knife, I cut into the first round bread labelled '*pain au levain*' which I determined from its tangy flavour to be the infamous sourdough. I remembered my father making a sourdough starter at home, and leaving it to ferment overnight. I used to love watching it transform and come to life.

"See the bubbles, Edie?" he used to say. That means wild yeast from the air and the flour itself have started making themselves a home in your starter. They will eat the sugars in the flour and increase the acidity of the mixture, preventing other 'bad' microbes from growing."

It was like a delicious science experiment. Once the sourdough became frothy and fermented, it was ready to use. My mother insisted he keep his 'experiments' in the utility room because of the strong, pungent smell. He would then bake a loaf of yummy bread (which went a long way towards making up for the stink) then hold back a portion of the sourdough, 'feed' it with flour and water, and keep the process going. He said some bakers would have kept a sourdough "mother" going for more than 100 years. I used to think it was a bit strange at the time, growing bacteria to make bread, but tasting this light and airy loaf in the bakery made me truly appreciate this time-honoured tradition. It also made me wonder how old the Moreau's sourdough was and if that was the 'secret ingredient' that made their bread the best kept secret in northern France.

Next I tried a round '*pain aux raisins*' which I knew to be raisin bread. I instinctively tapped on the base of the loaf, hearing a wonderfully deep echo that sounded the guarantee of a thick, dark crust. The crunchy bread was tantalisingly good and the sweet, swollen raisins gave it an extra dimension. After a large glass of milk, I gluttonously moved on to a wholesome '*pain aux noix*', a walnut bread made with whole-wheat flour. In France, the walnut was the king of the nuts, so they simply referred to this loaf as nut bread, as if walnut is the only nut worth eating. With just the right balance of acidity and crunchy walnuts were almost whole (meaning they must have been added after the kneading process) this bread was my favourite. Moist and slightly darker in colour than the others, I could have happily gorged on the entire loaf. Of course I ate them all like a true Irish girl and smothered butter all over them. By the time I got to the '*pain bis*', a rye bread, I was completely stuffed and full of respect for our reclusive baker. I wasn't an expert or anything, but from the flavours and textures of the breads, it confirmed my suspicions that they were baked in a wood-burning oven. I pushed back my chair and looked towards the rear of the shop. There was a swinging door that led to a small room with a sink and a small worktop for preparing *tartines* or sandwiches and a little electric *chauffe grille* for toasting.

Without consciously making a plan, I got up and strolled over towards the back, fixing things and wiping counters as I passed. I looked back out onto the street, which was quiet at this time of day and listened out for any sound of Mme Moreau upstairs. I could just about hear her little television, no doubt showing one of those ghastly chat shows where dancing girls just prance around topless for no apparent reason. Satisfied that I would not be disturbed, I sneaked into the kitchenette. I had seen a tiny door there before, just beside the miniature fridge, but had simply assumed it was a cupboard, such was the size. It was painted a pale eggshell blue/grey colour, with two panels of frosted glass obscuring what lay beyond. But now I realised that what lay beyond must be the basement. Mme Moreau, being small in stature, would have easily fit through, but I would have to crouch. I gently turned the little glass knob, but to my disappointment, it was locked. I just stood there looking at it, willing it to open. Then inspiration struck, and I quickly swung the door of the kitchenette open again. The unisex toilet (which was an actual toilet, as opposed to a hole in the ground) was just on the other side of the kitchenette and although I wasn't sure what access could be gained from the loo, it was worth a try. The loo was quite posh as it goes, with some kind of vintage wallpaper, repeating scenes of the well-to-do taking part in various outdoor pursuits. The taps were gold plated, as was the mirror and it felt at once both homely and chic.

To my delight, I spotted a grille plate on the floor behind the sink that looked down into the basement. An old iron thing, I lifted it easily with my pen and for the first time I had a partial view of the baker's domain. It was incredibly authentic and I realised that things must have changed very little since Monsieur Moreau's time. The walls were simply exposed bricks and the floor a plain concrete, and everything was dusted with a fine layer of flour. No wonder the bread tasted so good, I mused, they were probably using age-old recipes and baking them in the wood fire oven. I could just see the side of it from my rather awkward vantage point, but I didn't even need to – I could smell the rich scent of burnt wood. I could just make out the bags of flour stacked against the wall marked '*Farine*' and tall wooden shelves holding antique moulds and sheet pans, slightly warped from the intense heat of the ovens. The only thing missing was the baker himself, but I assumed he must have finished for the day, as he would have started baking at 4 am. My knees were hurting, kneeling down on the tiled floor and I was about to heave myself up when a voice startled me.

"*Eh, ça va Édith*?" asked Manu, clearly bewildered by my behaviour.

"Oh Manu, I didn't see you there," I replied a little flustered. "I, eh, just lost my earring" I bluffed, "*j'ai perdu* my earring," I repeated, laughing at my own stupidity and sliding the grate back into place with my foot. He just nodded, but I knew he wasn't convinced. I just had time to tidy up after my little taster session when Mme Moreau reappeared, unceremoniously turning off the music. She seemed irritated, which was nothing new, but something about the music had affected her. There was no time to question her, as it was time to open up again and I needed to run upstairs to freshen myself up. Climbing the stairs, I still couldn't shake the feeling that Manu and Mme Moreau's inimical façade was an attempt to hide something. But what? Were they really doing something illegal down there? It hardly seemed likely. But I could tell from their strange behaviour that something was going on and I was determined to get to the bottom of it.

***

That evening I met Nicole for a drink in a café overlooking the river. Walking down the lamp lit streets, and taking the familiar turns towards the city centre, I realised that Compiègne had indeed become familiar to me. Had it really only been a week since I arrived on that unexpected train journey from Paris, full of disappointment at my sheer bad luck to have taken on a job in some outlying village? It seemed like a lifetime ago and while I was hardly a local yet, I had come a long way in one short week. Nicole was sitting at the bar chatting amiably with one of the bar staff when I arrived. I had never met someone so comfortable in their own skin and the ease with which she bonded with people left me feeling a little envious.

"So…" she prompted, after ordering me a glass of wine and a snack of pate and bread. Both were exceedingly delicious and bursting with strong flavours.

"So, he… I mean Hugo walked me home," I began, though it felt strange saying his name out loud. It was such a magical night and while I had tried my hardest not to daydream about it since, I sometimes wondered if it had ever happened at all.

"Yes, and…" she said impatiently.

"Well we talked a lot and oh, you know he's a photographer?" I said.

"*Très bien, et…*" she prompted, eager to get to the good bits.

"Okay okay, we kissed!" I giggled like a schoolgirl and didn't even have the dignity to hide it. The memory of his soft lips came rushing back to me and I actually blushed. "God he was such a good kisser."

"*Voilà – je l'avais dis*! You're going to have fun in France, non?" she squealed. "Are you meeting him again?"

"Well that's just it; he said he had to go to Toulouse for something or other. Oh and his mother lives there, so. Actually, I don't know when he's coming back, he didn't say."

"Did he take your number? I'm sure he'll call," she said matter-of-factly, flipping her dark hair over her shoulder and revealing giant white hoop earrings.

"Eh, no he didn't," I realised with a sinking feeling. "I didn't even think to ask."

"Hmm, but he lives here right?"

"I don't know that either!" I realised with a shock. "What's wrong with me, why didn't I ask him the most basic of questions?" I asked, realising that he hadn't offered the information either. "Oh God, you don't think he's married do you?"

"*Pourquoi*, what makes you think that?" Nicole asked, clearly less concerned about the possibility than me. She was French after all.

"Well, when we got back to the bakery, I invited him up and he just said something about having to get up early. At the time I thought he was being chivalrous, you know? I mean I'm not completely deluded, I'm sure he was interested, but it's like he stopped himself. Now I'm thinking it was guilt that made him hesitate."

"*Non, je ne pense pas*. He did not have that vibe of a married man."

"What vibe?" I asked.

"Well, it's hard to describe, but he was too uneasy to be married. You know, married men are just more relaxed, probably because they know they have someone at home. Nah, he was too tense to be married."

"That's ridiculous, tense people get married. Relaxed people marry and become tense! What kind of reasoning is that? You're just trying to spare my feelings."

"Maybe," she admitted. "But look, there are so many other men here," her gaze took in a room full of couples.

I titled my head with an ironic look.

"Okay well not *here* here, but why are you putting all your apples in this basket?"

"It's eggs," I corrected her.

"*N'importe quoi*," she sighed, exasperated. "You really like him, *hein*?"

I nodded helplessly.

"Perhaps he was being, how did you say, chivalrous? He is part English after all."

I gulped the rest of my wine with a hard swallow. "He was such a good kisser," I repeated, looking out the window.

"Tell me about it again," she encouraged me and I did, until I was smiling again and fairly sure that I would hear from him again.

When I got home that night and let myself into my little apartment, I noticed something on the mat as I opened the door. Picking it up, I realised that it was a postcard with pictures of red-tiled rooftops. I flipped it over and straight away saw the name 'Hugo' signed at the end. My heart skipped as I threw off my coat and sat on the bed to read it properly.

Miss Lane,
Still dreaming a little dream of you
Hugo x

Short, sweet and incandescently romantic. He hadn't asked for my number, but he had remembered my address. There was something so wonderfully old-fashioned about sending a postcard, rather than texting me. 'God he's smooth', I thought to myself, for he now had me hook, line and sinker.

Chapter 12

I couldn't sleep that night. At home in Dublin, I often had
sleepless nights after Mum passed away. This was due in part
to the fact that I didn't want to dream about her, only to wake
and find her not there. But the restlessness I felt here was
caused by a very different set of emotions. I smiled happily to
myself when I thought of how pleased my mother would be,
seeing me not only living my life, but living my crazy dreams.
That was her only wish; that I would not remain closed off
from the world.

"You will be sad, of course you will, but in time you will
have to get on with your life, Edie," she told me, somehow
holding back the tears.

What can you say, except yes, I will carry on. But when she
died, all I felt was anger. How could she expect me to be
strong and stoic, like she had always been? I wanted to be
that person for her, but it was all a facade. What I really felt
was scared. The last few years were like living suspended in
mid-air, always waiting for the other shoe to drop. She
couldn't have known how that felt for me and at the time, my
feelings didn't seem important anyway. She was the one who
was suffering, not me.

Those memories would have haunted me once, but here, in
this place, I felt different. Perhaps I was moving through
those other stages of grief, the ones that brought you closer to
acceptance. Maybe I was beginning to understand myself a
little better. I abandoned my squeaking mattress and got up to
make a hot chocolate. On seeing that I was out of milk, I
decided to go downstairs to make it, figuring I would be less
likely to wake Mme Moreau. With my dressing gown

wrapped tightly around me against the chill of the old building, I put on a saucepan of milk and checked the wall clock in the kitchen. Almost four o'clock and little or no sleep; I knew I would struggle today, but somehow it didn't really matter. As I poured the warm cocoa flavoured milk with a little cinnamon into a large bowl, I sat at the counter and wrapped my hands around it. It took a little while for me to realise that the far off noises echoing underneath me were voices. Voices? I strained to hear by lifting my head and turning it to one side, just like a dog and confirmed that yes, I could hear two people speaking. But it wasn't coming from the street outside, it was coming from the basement.

'Of course', I said, shaking my head at my own stupidity, 'there are two bakers'. I took a refreshing sip of my hot chocolate as my thought processes figured it all out. It was nearly four o'clock in the morning and they must have just begun burning the wood in the ovens, while they started the day's baking. It made perfect sense now. One was in charge of the breads, the other of the pastries. I knew it was too much work for one person. But then I heard her. Mme Moreau's guttural discourses were unmistakable. But what on earth was she doing down there?

I launched myself towards the bathroom door and deftly lifted the grate by the sink, through which I had spied the basement the day before. It was difficult to see anything at first, the light was so dim. I could feel the warm air rising from the ovens and that sour smell of yeast proving and turning plain old flour and water into something magical. With a shuffling of feet, Manu came into view, wearing a white apron around his waist and his sleeves rolled up.

'So he is making an apprenticeship', I remarked, a little surprised. It took a lot of time and dedication to become a top baker and at 15 it seemed an ambitious undertaking. In an odd way I felt sort of proud of him. I know nothing would have got me out of bed at four am when I was his age, or any age for that matter. I couldn't see Mme Moreau, but I could hear her giving orders.

"*Maintenant, tu fais exactement comme lui,*" she said, directing him to do exactly as the baker was doing.

Standing by the large table that ran the full length of the wall, he began kneading a large pillow of dough and I tried to follow his eye line to see if I could spot the head baker. At first, I couldn't see anything; he seemed to be staring straight at the ovens. Gradually, a strange feeling came over me; a heaviness that had not been there moments earlier. Then I began to notice a flicker… once, twice. What I saw that night turned my blood to ice. A man, if you could call him that, stood side by side with Manu, except he had no feet and seemed to be standing in mid-air. That was when I fainted.

***

I awoke in my bed with absolutely no recollection of how I had gotten there. I had a terrible headache and my body felt bruised and sore. With a terrible fright, I recalled the image of the man in the basement. Though rationally, I supposed it could have all been a dream, the result of an overactive imagination. I reached for my phone and almost pole-vaulted out of bed when I saw that it was gone eight o'clock. I pulled on a t-shirt and jeans and popped my feet into a pair of pumps, before thundering down the stairs and yanking my layered locks into a pony tail. I burst into the bakery with such a force that I almost ran into Monsieur Raynard, a kind elderly gentleman who came in for his coffee and *tartine* every morning.

"*Oh, excusez-moi!*" I flushed and he kindly said the fault was entirely his for standing in front of the door. They just didn't make them like that anymore (although secretly I hoped they did).

I was prepared to beg forgiveness from Mme Moreau for my tardiness, but to my complete shock, she cut me off by saying that Manu had already made my excuses and that she hoped my headache had improved.

"Erm, yes ... thanks," was all I could muster, before putting on my apron and getting stuck into the usual tasks. But as the day wore on, it became clear that Manu and I would have to have words.

***

I called my Dad that afternoon when I took my coffee break. Choosing my favourite *croissant aux amandes* with its yummy frangipane centre, I sat outside at a little square around the corner as the afternoon sunshine warmed my face.

"Happy birthday!" I cheered, trying to make up for the fact that I wouldn't be there for his birthday.

"Ah Edie, how are ya love? I got me card – didn't understand a word of it," he laughed.

"I'm sorry I'm not there Dad, but I hope you're keeping up the tradition." Every year for his birthday we would go to Bewleys Café for tea and cake as a little treat.

"Would you believe your aunty Gemma arrived up this morning and frog-marched me into town? Sure I'd forgotten all about it," he said.

God bless aunt Gemma, I thought. My father's sister was the one who had kept us afloat after Mum died, constantly calling over with food, enthusiasm and love. She was younger than him by about ten years and had her own family of three boys to look after, but she was the best aunt, sister, counsellor and friend that we could have asked for.

"Anyway, how are them frogs treating ya?" he asked.

"I don't think it's politically correct to say that anymore," I reproved.

"Well, I'm sure they called us worse. So, have you made any friends over there yet?"

I filled him in on Nicole and her family and he sounded genuinely reassured that there were people looking out for his not-so-little girl. I didn't mention Hugo, or things that go bump in the night, even though I wanted to, badly. There was just no way to ask someone, 'Do you believe in ghosts?' without sounding like a nutter.

I wished him all the best for his special day and promised to call again soon. I kept to myself at the bakery that afternoon, focusing all of my attention on our patrons while keeping my distance from Mme Moreau. I waited for Manu to return that evening, but Mme Moreau insisted I knock off early, saying she thought I looked a little pale. I couldn't understand her change in attitude, but I was rather tired and I had a mountain of laundry to get through before bed. I had put off the '*lavage*' since my arrival, as it appeared there was no washing machine in the building and this meant spending hours in a launderette.

After lugging what felt like a dead body around on my back, I found one open near the university campus and dumped my sports bag on the counter. The noise of the machines droned mercilessly, as comatose students sat watching their clothes circumnavigate the drum. It was self-service, so I separated the lights and darks and put money in the two machines. After five minutes of watching them spin, a flashing sign across the street caught my eye. It was an Internet café, probably geared towards the student population, but being a

84

mature student in the university of life, I thought I'd fit right in.

My fears of eviction for being too old were unfounded, as I found people from all age groups sitting in front of the screens. An extremely cute guy who was ten years too young for me, nodded at me from the rear of the shop to take a seat at one of the free stations. A sign explained that the charge was €2 per hour, a steal. Faced with the search engine, I didn't know what to type. 'What do ghosts look like?' or 'Do ghosts exist?' seemed too broad a search, but I had to start somewhere.

Sure enough, the results flooded the screen. I read some spooky accounts of hearing footsteps by your door or windows opening by themselves. I was never one for watching scary movies and I felt the hairs rise on the back of my neck with fear. Then I was greeted by some terrifying images of ghosts walking along a landing in an old castle and I actually shrieked. 'This is stupid', I told myself, and shut the screen down. Instead, I opened my email and wrote to aunt Gemma to thank her for making Dad's birthday special. I also filled her in on French life and how I still hoped to visit Paris properly once I found the time. I paid the cute guy (getting a wink for my trouble) and went back to transfer my clothes to the drier. Sitting there with nothing to distract me, I began to feel terribly lonely. My thoughts inevitably turned to Hugo, despite my attempts to not think of him. Though we only had one night together, I felt as though I knew him intimately. Why the hell didn't I get his number? With that, the drier thudded and clicked to a halt and it was time to start folding.

That night, I got into bed early with a hot water bottle I had bought at the chemist. It brought some comfort against the cold and I drifted off to sleep quite easily. But just before four o'clock, I woke and sat up rigid in the bed. My dreams had been full of eerie images and phantom noises. I felt convinced that there was someone standing outside my door. All was quiet now and I was about to lie back down under the covers when my stereo came to life, playing my Django Reinhardt CD. Had I been a cat, I would have been hanging from the ceiling by my claws. I didn't dare breathe, but as suddenly as it came on, the stereo went silent. After some tense moments of negotiation with myself, I dared to reach my hand out from under the sheet and switch on the lamp. Everything sat motionless and ordinary, as it should be. I slowly began to allow myself to breathe again and took the courageous step to get out of bed and plug out the stereo, only to find that it was in fact, never plugged in. Feeling faint again, I grabbed a chair and sat there for a long time.

My first instinct was to pack. I could toss my clothes into a bag in less than five minutes and get out of there. Get the early morning train to Paris and take a standby flight home from the airport. Yet, I didn't move. My second thought was to go to Mme Moreau's apartment, banging on the door and demanding answers. Yet, I didn't do that either. I just sat there, thinking of my mother. I hadn't realised it earlier, at the Internet café, but things had changed dramatically in my life and so my perception of everything else had altered too. Ghosts were no longer just clichéd poltergeists from scary movies. Ghosts were people once. The fear had all but drained away, so I got up, put on my dressing gown and went down the stairs.

Chapter 13

How wrong could I have been; I was terrified. The fleeting courage I had found immediately deserted me. I mean, who goes out of their way to meet a ghost? Crouching in my usual space below the sink (light years from my Parisian dream) I lifted the grate and searched below for any sign of life – or death as the case may be. Again, I could hear Manu and Mme Moreau's voices; hers a low hum of encouragement, his, an excited chattering. I began to have my doubts about the 'presence' I had seen the other night, for they seemed to be alone. Then, just as before, a flickering image appeared by Manu's side and I thought I would pass out again. I had to concentrate on my breathing, trying to slow it down and as I did, I prayed to my mother for courage and understanding. I tried to remember what I had felt upstairs in my room – this person was alive once. Just a normal person with their own hopes and fears. I held my hand on my chest and felt my heart rate begin to decelerate. As I began to calm down a little, I lay flat on the ground (which, in a toilet, is a huge sacrifice of personal hygiene) to get a better look. The man, for he was dressed like a man, appeared almost like a hologram. His opaqueness was lit by some unseen light source, so he sort of glowed, but dimly. I tried not to focus on the fact that he still had no feet and seemed to be hovering, and instead I switched my attention to what he was doing. To my amazement, he appeared to be in the process of kneading bread. There was no dough in his hands and he didn't appear to be touching anything, but his actions were that of a baker kneading and knocking the air out of the dough. It was then I noticed Manu mimicking every move that he was making, the only difference being that Manu was actually handling real live dough.

Then I heard Mme Moreau speak from the shadows.

"That's it, now you will be able to bake bread like a true Moreau!" she said, her voice breaking with pride, or sadness, or both.

I stayed there for another quarter hour, having brought my trusty notebook to take notes so I wouldn't be second-guessing myself later. I had to plan my next move very carefully. It was clear that Manu knew what I was doing in the toilet that night and yet as far as I knew, he had said nothing to Mme Moreau. In a way, I inferred that he wanted me to find out, but as to why, I did not know. I would not confront them until I did a little digging of my own. While, living above a haunted bakery might take a little getting used to, I wasn't prepared to run away just yet.

***

I waited for him till the end of the day, when the street lamps popped on one by one and he returned to the bakery on his scooter. As was his routine, he began emptying all the leftover bread into a box for delivery to the homeless shelter.

"Why don't I go with you?" I suggested. By this stage I was accustomed to their complete lack of enthusiasm regarding anything I said. If there was one thing I had learned in this country, it was to just barge your way through instead of waiting for an invite.

Manu sort of sniffed and looked out at the scooter. He had a point; I couldn't see myself riding on the handlebars.

"Why don't we walk, eh *marchez*? I'm sure it's pas loin. It's not too far, is it Mme Moreau and I can help to carry some of the boxes." Instead of her usual shrug, I almost detected what might have been considered a smile. Perhaps I was breaking down her walls after all and with that, off we trudged through the cobbled streets.

"So, you're interested in becoming a baker then?" I asked, starting the proceedings with a little small talk.

"*Oui.*"

"And you are learning from the baker I saw in the basement last night?" I let the sentence hang there until he worked it out.

"You saw... 'im? He asked a little hesitantly.

"I saw something and I definitely wasn't dreaming," I said, matching his frankness. "*Ce n'était pas un rêve.*"

"*S'il vous plaît...* do not speak of last night to Mme Moreau," he blurted, in surprisingly good English for his age. The school system over here obviously put far more emphasis on languages than our own at home.

Up until that moment, I doubted my own sanity. Each time that image of Monsieur Moreau standing there (or hovering there) crept up, I felt slightly weak and had spent the entire day after explaining it away. Lack of sleep, a play of shadows, even having a nervous breakdown seemed a preferable alternative to what I knew in my gut to be true.

"I'm not sure what I saw," I replied honestly "but I think I deserve an explanation".

Neither of us spoke for a while. Manu led the way and took a right turn by the side of a large church I hadn't seen before. At the back, there was something of a hall with a line of windows lit up warmly from the inside and a queue of people extending out the door. Manu greeted some of the people in the queue and quite gentlemanly, let me go in ahead of him. I hadn't really thought about where we were going, my mind was so fixed on getting answers out of him. But now that we had arrived, I was both surprised and humbled by what I saw.

It was like a canteen with lots of tables set up for dinner and at the top of the room there was a counter manned by volunteers handing out bowls of steaming soup and a main of some kind of casserole. A priest spotted Manu and came out from behind the counter to greet us.

"*Bonjour Emanuelle*," he greeted him, making me snigger as it sounded like such a girl's name. "*T'as amené une petite amie?*"

"*Père Bernard, je vous présente Mademoiselle Lane,*" Manu spoke respectfully. "*Elle est irlandaise*," he added almost as an excuse for any upcoming blunders I would make.

In that vein, I wasn't entirely sure of the etiquette and whether or not I was supposed to kiss him, but thankfully, as I put the boxes down on a table, he took my hand and shook it. It didn't help that I suddenly forgot all my French, which I was wont to do on social occasions, but again he took the initiative.

"*Ça vous plaît, la vie ici en France?*"

"*Oh oui, je suis très contente ici,*" I rhymed off, though it did feel wrong lying to a priest. "This place is amazing," I said, nodding at Manu to translate for me.

"Father says, it is our *responsibilité* to protect the forgotten," Manu said, filling in the blanks for me.

And these people were forgotten. Many of them looked foreign, with dark skin and brown eyes, just like Manu and Mme Moreau. As we walked back to the bakery, I had a whole new set of questions for Manu.

"Those people back there," I began, "they're not French, are they?"

He eyed me up for a moment before answering. "Roma," was all he said.

"And you and Mme Moreau?"

He just nodded in response.

"Are you related?" I pressed on, aware that this was really none of my business, but at the same time, I felt as though I was being drawn into something and had a right to know.

"*C'est ma grand-mère*," he said.

"Grandmother?" I repeated unnecessarily. I let it sink in for a while. I couldn't understand why they hadn't just told me that in the beginning. Perhaps something had happened to Manu's parents, Mme Moreau's son or daughter and that was why she was looking after Manu. And as for their background, I knew nothing about Roma gypsies or their culture. All I knew from Ireland was the traveller culture and how interaction between the settled and travelling communities was usually complicated. They seemed to be caught in a catch 22, because the government wanted them to settle and fit in with everybody else, but then nobody wanted them to settle next door. There was a lack of trust on both sides, suspicion and misunderstanding. It must have been the same here.

"So, can you tell me what really happened last night? Does it happen every night?"

He was obviously uncomfortable talking about it, but he seemed more concerned about me blabbing my suspicions to Mme Moreau, rather than what I would do with the information. Still, he was guarded.

"It's okay Manu," I said, feeling a rush of maternal feeling towards him. "*Vous n'êtes pas obligé de tout me dire maintenant*, we can talk about it later," I assured him. It was clear he wasn't ready to talk to me about it and I wasn't sure how ready I was to hear it. It was enough to know that I wasn't going crazy and Mme Moreau's secret was safe between us for the time being. On that mutual ground, we parted for the night, but my curiosity still tugged at me. I couldn't help but wonder where or rather when, the apparition was coming from. Had something happened in the towns' history, or perhaps the building itself?

'One too many episodes of Most Haunted and you think you're a medium!' I joked with myself.

Come to think of it, there was always a common thread running through that TV show; you had to explore the history of a place to really understand what was going on. Besides, it wouldn't hurt to find out a bit more about Compiègne's past and so I made the decision to call Geoff, the English tour guide with a taste for éclairs, the following day.

Chapter 14

We arranged to meet at his home that Sunday, which was in a small suburb across the River Oise. Ruby had taken the dogs out for a walk – a whippet and a bulldog aptly named Little and Large. It was the first time I had seen a regular French suburban house and it struck me as being quite plain but at the same time exotic, when compared to Irish houses. It was a little bungalow, perfect for the two of them, he informed me.

"We don't have extravagant tastes, just as long as the dogs are happy and I have room for my books, I'm alright anywhere."

I wondered if Ruby shared his Buddhist sense of detachment.

"Do you ever miss home? I asked him, as we contorted ourselves into his micro-sized Smart car.

"Oh you know, we get back now and again. Ruby has to get her tea and bread from Marks, but to be fair, you can pick that up in Paris. We don't have any children and there's just Ruby's Mum left now. She's in a home in Bristol."

"I hope Ruby won't mind me stealing you for the day - did she not want to come?"

"Her exact words were, 'If I have to suffer through another one of your tours, we're getting a divorce', so no, I don't think she'll mind in the least. But tell me, what made you decide to come? I didn't think a young girl like you would have much interest in war museums," he remarked, starting the engine.

"Well, it's not so much the war aspect that I'm interested in. I'd just like to know more about the history of the place, that's all," I replied. Not to mention the context in which a man would have died and begun reappearing at my bakery. I wasn't even sure if anything Geoff could tell me would offer any clues about this mysterious man, but I didn't really know where else to start the search.

We drove east out of Compiègne on the N31. It felt strange leaving the city and seeing the outskirts for the first time. Rue De Paris had become my entire world since I arrived; so much so that I had almost forgotten that there was an entire country to be explored. Within minutes, we were driving into the Compiègne Forest. It was beautiful, so peaceful and verdant. Passing by the massive Alsace Lorraine Monument -- a huge sculpture depicting a sword cutting down the Imperial Eagle of Germany, it became clear to me why so many war historians held this place in such high regard. We parked in a small car park and walked along a wooded path to an extraordinary clearing. In front of us lay railway tracks leading to the centre of the memorial. To one side there was a statue of Marshal Foch and ahead, between a tank and a gun, stood the museum; a nondescript, low, white building with flags fluttering in the breeze.

Although the area itself was green and lush and smelled of sap, there was a sense of something solemn that had taken place. Even though I was, as yet, incognizant of what had happened in this place, I could sense the gravity of it. We entered the small building and Geoff explained that this was the Armistice Museum. He purchased our tickets and went into full tour guide mode and despite myself, I was hooked on his every word. He looked the part too, in his mustard corduroy trousers and v-neck jumper.

"Now Edith, this is a replica of the railway carriage used by Marshal Foch and his officers, who included the English First Lord of the Admiralty, Sir Rosslyn Wemyss, and the French Chief of Staff, General Weygand. It was here that they met with the Germans to sign the Armistice to end the horror that

94

was World War I. It was signed on November 11th at 5.10am."

"And who was Marshal Foch when he was at home?" I asked.

"Basically, he was the Commander-in-chief of the Allied Armies. The head honcho. He was revered as a great military theorist and fought the Germans back into their own territory. He did predict however that the armistice was not a permanent peace and that after 20 years, war could break out once again. He was right; 20 years and 65 days later, the Second World War began."

It was chilling, not like history lessons at school where books containing old photos of dead generals did little to convey the realities of war. There was a lot of World War 1 memorabilia in that room with yellowing newspaper articles, photocopies, old cameras showing pictures from the various fronts, flags, objects made from shells, old hypnotic film footage that flickered and eerily reminded me of the ghostly baker.

For such a small museum, the atmosphere was extraordinary. The simplicity of the display and the objects was so affecting, drawing visitors into those past events.

"What about World War II?" I asked. I wasn't sure what age my ghost was or when he lived (although I made an instant note to myself to stop calling him 'my ghost'). For some reason however, I had a strange hunch that this was the time period I should be focussing on.

"I'm coming to that just now Madame."

"It's Mademoiselle!" I replied. "Everyone rather rudely assumes I should be paired off by now," I said, a little testily.

"Maybe they just find it hard to believe you haven't been snapped up yet," he said.

"Snapped up? I'm not a cut-price loaf sitting on a shelf, waiting to be 'snapped up'! I replied, clicking my fingers. "Still, I'll take your feeble attempt at a compliment Sir and move you swiftly back to the history lesson."

"Okay, okay, hold fire," he joked, holding up his hands and we continued with the tour.

He really came into his own when talking about the past – you could tell it was his passion and I felt really lucky to have this knowledgeable guide all to myself.

"Right, so this space covers the events of 1940, which was a very different story for the French. The Battle of France was lost; the enemy was in Paris and France was about to be cut in half. A request for an armistice was made, and here in the forest at what was called the Glade of the Armistice, the French and German delegations met on June 21st, 1940. Talks were conducted in the very railway carriage that had been the scene of Germany's defeat. Then the Armistice was agreed –- a deliberate and highly effective venue for French humiliation. " He paused to let the significance of the site sink in.

"During the German occupation of France, from 1940 to 1944, the site was cleared and the carriage taken to Berlin. Later as the war went badly for Germany, it was moved to the forest of Thuringe and destroyed by fire in April 1945.

This wasn't the end of the story for the forest clearing known as the Glade of the Armistice. On September 1st, 1944, Compiègne was liberated. In November, General Marie-Pierre Koenig, the best known Free French leader after General de Gaulle, led a military parade in the Glade watched by crowds that included British, American and Polish officials".

"Wow, so this place really played a pivotal role in France's history," I said.

"Now she gets it!" he jeered, "don't I keep telling you that you haphazardly picked one of the most important locations in all of Europe! And that's why I'm kept very busy with tourists who want to come here and see it for themselves. In fact, on November 11th, 1950, a replica railway-carriage was officially opened containing the objects that you see today."

We spent some time walking around and quietly absorbing the exhibit. I could hear American accents as well as British and Italian. I was a bit embarrassed at how clueless I was about the whole thing; what the war really meant for the French who shared their border with the enemy. I thanked Geoff for being such an engaging tour guide and promised that there would be plenty of éclairs in it for him.

"Before we go back to town, I must show you one more thing," he said.

Back in the little Smart Car, which was surprisingly nippy and refreshingly silent, I let my window down and enjoyed the fragrant woodland breeze on my face.

"Maybe I should get a car," I mused, "it's nice to get out into the countryside."

"Well, you don't really need a car to get around. Ruby and me just used our bicycles when we first arrived. It's much more cycle-friendly weather than back home in Britain, and you can bring them on the trains too."

"Gosh, I haven't cycled in years," I said "I'm not sure I'd remember how!"

"It's easy - just like riding a bike," Geoff winked.

"You've really got to work on your material Geoff," I laughed, comfortable in his company.

As we travelled along the main road, Geoff pulled the car over to what appeared to be a forest path. We walked along until we reached a gravestone. I looked at him questioningly.

"It marks the spot of the last train from Compiègne to Buchenwald on August 17th, 1944, carrying 1,250 men to the death camp."

"What? You mean, trains left from here for the concentration camps in Germany?" I couldn't believe the words I was saying. German occupation, Nazis, the holocaust, these were things that were a million miles away from my life.

"In fact there was an internment camp here that held many Jews and French resistance soldiers. They detained them here and eventually shipped them off to the labour camps where most of them perished."

I felt numb with shock. This place seemed so peaceful; it was impossible to imagine such traumatic events had taken place here. The stark realisation affected me deeply and I could feel the tears welling up in my eyes. Geoff kindly handed me a tissue and when I had composed myself, I asked him how he could bear coming here, time after time.

"People need to remember Edith, otherwise their deaths and the thousands of people who sacrificed their lives trying to protect them, will have been for nothing."

His words were so powerful. Remembrance was the best way to honour people.

"My mother would have loved to come to France," I said.

He paused for a while, then took out a pack of cigarettes. I had never smoked in my life, but for some reason it seemed like the right thing to do in this instance. I coughed and wheezed as he lit it for me and I tried, unsuccessfully, to inhale. He lit his own and slowly gathered his thoughts.

"She's no longer with us, is she?"

"No," I replied, glad that I didn't have to explain.

"Is that why you're here?"

"I don't know, maybe." I realised that that was a question I hadn't been able to answer myself.

"Tell you what, why don't I show you some place that both you and your mother would have really loved?" he said, patting my arm. He reminded me a bit of my own father and that wasn't just the seventies sideburns. He had a no-nonsense attitude that made him easy to be around. "It's not far," he assured me.

We headed back towards the city centre as the sun began its descent into soft, lavender clouds. Just as he had promised, it did not take long before we entered another car park, but this time we were at the entrance to a grand castle, set in stately gardens and surrounded by woodland.

"What is this place?" I said, shaking off the shadows of the forest.

"This," he said, taking off his seatbelt, "is where I bring all the wives when they get fed up following their husbands around all the war museums. It seems to do the trick," he said casually.

I was completely taken aback by the scale of the castle. As we walked up the steps to the terrace, lined with magnificent classical statues, I mentioned to Geoff that it kind of resembled Buckingham Palace.

"There are similarities, yes. Indeed, Château Compiègne is an example of the First French Empire style from the 18th century, but the Compiègne estate dates back to the Merovingian Dynasty." He was back in tour guide mode and again I found myself grateful to have his fountain of knowledge on tap, if I could just keep up with what he was talking about.

"The who Dynasty?"

"In the 5th Century, the Merovingian dynasty ruled the Franks in a region known in Latin as Francia (an area made up of ancient Gaul and several Roman provinces) for 300 years. It's believed that all French kings descended from them."

"Wow, that's a lot of history. So who lived in the castle then?"

"Well, this area had always been popular among the royals, in fact it was a royal seat of government, but the Castle itself was built as a royal residence for Louis XV and was later restored by Napoleon. Even before the château was constructed, Compiègne was the preferred summer residence for French monarchs, primarily for hunting - given its proximity to Compiègne Forest."

"You're kidding me? I had no idea Compiègne was so… important! To think, I was so upset because I wouldn't be living in Paris," I told him.

"Oh no Edith, anyone who's anyone comes to Compiègne," he said in a high pitched tone that I think was meant to emulate his wife, Ruby.

"Oh dear, what time is it? I've taken up your Sunday afternoon, Ruby will kill me" I thought a little belatedly.

"You're joking right? She'll be delighted to have the house to herself. What she won't forgive me for is coming to the Château without her – she loves it here, all the paintings and the gardens – so you'll have to promise me you'll come here with her some day and experience her rather long-winded art history lessons."

"Art history?" I asked.

"Yes, she's a former art teacher and every woman I've brought here 'simply dies' when they visit the Second Empire museum – it's full of Empress Eugénie's clothing and marriage paraphernalia."

I'd love to come here again," I said, genuinely. I could see the long avenues leading off into the forest in the distance and could just imagine the Royals hunting on horseback and having a jolly old time of it.

"Right now, back to the Castle," he said as we walked around the grounds.

The building itself was spread out over a large area of about five hectares and was indeed very grand, but not as fussy as the pictures I had seen of Versailles or other French chateaus.

"No, it was built in a Neoclassical style, and what is Neoclassical style you might ask? It's when simplicity and clarity govern the design of both the external and interior features. In 1750, the prominent architect Ange-Jacques Gabriel proposed a thorough renovation of the château. During the French Revolution, the château passed into the jurisdiction of the Minister for the Interior. In 1795 all furniture was sold and its works of art were sent to the Muséum Central; it was essentially gutted. However, in 1804 Napoleon made the château an imperial domain and in 1807 he ordered it be made habitable again. Its layout was altered, a ballroom added, and the garden was replanted and linked directly to the forest. They say that 'Compiègne speaks of Napoleon as Versailles does of Louis XIV'. "

"Bravo!" I cheered, impressed by what seemed to be Geoff's photographic memory.

As we strolled around the gardens, the enormous Château and its extensive grounds put my own life into perspective. There was so much history there, centuries of Kings and Queens, life and death and yet it was the building and the forests that remained. It called to mind the figure I had seen in the bakery. I wasn't sure how to put it, other than blurting it out.

"Geoff, do you believe that places like this, with all their history, do you think they could be haunted?" I tried to say it casually, conversationally.

"What, do you mean ghosts?"

"Maybe, you know, or just I don't know, like a presence of some sort?"

"I don't really believe in all that palaver, but I suppose somewhere as old as this must have the odd ghost rattling about. I've heard stories," he added "on the old battlefields, but that could be just be a load of old twaddle!"

I nodded and didn't mention it further. It felt good to get away from the bakery for the day, but there was something drawing me back there – a mystery that needed to be solved.

Chapter 15

Another postcard arrived first thing Monday morning. I just about managed to refrain from kissing the postman, for my heart leapt at the thought of Hugo and his intense eyes that sought to know me on that magical night. I had been intermittently going over that evening in my head, wishing things had turned out differently. Our premature goodbye had left me feeling as though I'd missed my chance, so these postcards kept my foolish hopes alive.

The picture this time was of a beautiful bridge called Pont Neuf, stretching over a large expanse of water, namely the Garonne River. On the back it simply said:

Thinking of you Miss Lane,

Hoping it wasn't all just a dream.

Hugo x

I knew I shouldn't have been so affected by his words, but I couldn't help it. I had a major crush on this guy and in a way, I had sort of resigned myself to whatever would result from it. A fling, a heartache, a lifelong relationship; either way I was bound to see it through. I cringed at how his handwriting piqued my curiosity even further. I was desperate to know more about him, to find out if he felt the same way I did. At the same time, there was also a sense of being overwhelmed by my feelings and that made me want to run and hide. As though she could sense a romance afoot, Nicole called into the bakery that morning for a quick chat.

"He is very, you know, 'old fashioned, with his postcards and calling you 'Miss Lane'," she said, sipping a quick espresso at the counter.

"I know, I think that's what's making this so unbearably romantic!" I agreed, rather enjoying the drama of it all.

"He still does not say when he's coming back," she added, flipping the postcard over in her hand.

I left the statement unanswered and popped some *pain au chocolat* into a brown paper bag for her to take back to the salon.

"You busy today?" I said, changing the subject.

"Super busy, but I wanted to tell you that Johnny is playing in Nostalgie on Thursday night, so you have to come, yes?"

"Oh great, but I won't be able to drink," I said, which garnered a puzzled look from Nicole. "I'm not drinking because I refuse to squat over a hole in the ground every time I need the loo!"

Laughing hysterically she added, "Ah my Irish friend, you do make me laugh," and left the bakery giggling to herself, with her pastries under her arm.

Mme Moreau was at the specialist that afternoon for her arthritis, so for the first time I was left in charge of the bakery. It felt wonderful. This was what I had imagined when I left for Paris all those weeks ago. Once again I brought down my own stereo and played my Django Reinhardt cd, which I had completely fallen in love with, and served the customers in an efficient yet relaxed manner. I felt completely in control and I so enjoyed being my own boss and not having Mme Moreau's constant presence like a long shadow over me. Since I discovered the 'goings on' in the basement, I had lost the urge to impress her or win her over and I knew she sensed the change in me. Our interactions were purely perfunctory and it worked better for both of us that way. Manu on the other hand was entirely different with me, and I with him. I could sense the weight of responsibility he felt having to hide the Moreaus' secret and I knew it was only a matter of time before he would come to search me out.

When I closed up that evening, I decided to go out for a bite to eat. Mme Moreau had not yet returned from her outing and I didn't feel entirely comfortable being in the building on my own. I went to the brasserie where I had met Nicole the previous week and sat at the back of the restaurant where there was a banquette. The staff was kept on their toes with a decent number of patrons eating out on a Monday night. I ordered a 'Salade Roquefort', a blue cheese and walnut salad that packed a punch, with a glass of equally bolshie red wine. That was one thing I was coming to appreciate about France – their ballsy flavours and simple presentation. Bread, wine and cheese could happily sustain the population for breakfast, lunch and dinner. I was so tired and preoccupied after a long day at work that I didn't really mind eating out on my own – something I never would have done at home in Dublin. I always thought people either looked lonely or ridiculously self-confident when eating out alone. I felt neither just now in my absentmindedness. A thought was forming in my subconscious, and it was only as I mopped up the dressing with my bread that it came to the fore.

"I'll Google him!" I actually said it aloud without realising, but thankfully no-one seemed to notice. I quickly paid my bill and carefully worked out the tip, which can be quite a challenge for someone allergic to percentages. Grabbing my coat, I set out for the Internet café I had used the other evening to see if I could find out a bit more about Hugo Chadwick.

Taking my place at a free station, I quickly typed 'Hugo Chadwick photographer' into the search engine. The first result was for a genealogy website, where a woman was searching for a Hugo Chadwick who had died in the late 1800's. The second was for a country pub in England called

The Chadwick Arms and after that there were a few photography studios in Australia and America with the name Chadwick, but nothing for my Hugo. I deleted the word 'photographer' and hit search once more. This time, the first result was a Facebook page for Hugo Chadwick. My heart jolted, then my conscience had a serious argument about looking too eager if I sent him a message and quite possibly ruining the old-fashioned correspondence we had going on. Still, I need not have wasted my energy worrying, for when I clicked on the link I found a black and white picture of a Colombian body builder. Not too hard on the eye, but still not my Hugo. I felt a bit deflated and hardly noticed the next link for Chadwick Holdings Incorporated. My eyes glanced over the first line or two, with words such as 'principal investor', 'commercial properties' and 'asset management', which held little or no meaning for me. Just out of curiosity, I noted that their registered office was in London with a subsidiary in Paris. Believing the entire enterprise to be idiotic and hopeless, I abandoned my background search for Hugo and sat back in the hard plastic chair wondering what else I could do to use up the hour.

I searched my email and found a response from Aunt Gemma. She was full of news about the boys and sounded so pleased that I was getting on well. I typed another quick message, telling her about my trip to the Armistice Memorial and the grand Château de Compiègne. Once the email was sent, I found myself, quite subconsciously, forming a new search. My fingers typed the words 'ghosts and hauntings'. My eyes ran down the page, searching for something reliable. After some browsing on the subject, I discovered that a lot of websites referred to two main types of hauntings; intelligent and residual. Something in my gut made me click on residual and when I spotted something called 'The Stone Tape' theory on Wikipedia, I opened it. The explanation I found was eerily accurate.

'The Stone Tape theory is a paranormal hypothesis that was proposed in the 1970s as a possible explanation for ghosts. It speculates that inanimate materials can absorb some form of energy from living beings; the hypothesis speculates that this "recording" happens especially during moments of high tension, such as murder, or during intense moments of someone's life. This stored energy can then be released, resulting in a display of the recorded activity. According to this hypothesis, ghosts are not spirits but simply non-interactive recordings similar to a movie. Paranormal investigators commonly consider such phenomena as residual hauntings.'

I shivered in my seat and rubbed my arms vigorously. Looking around the room and seeing other regular people sitting near me, just checking their emails or playing computer games made me feel a little less scared. I had never even heard of residual hauntings before, yet scientifically, it seemed like a more plausible explanation for what we would call hauntings. I read on:

'In the terminology of ghost hunting, residual hauntings are repeated playbacks of auditory, visual, olfactory, and other sensory phenomena that are attributed to a traumatic event, life-altering event, or a routine event of a person or place, like an echo or a replay of a videotape of past events. Ghost hunters and related paranormal television programs say that a residual haunting, unlike an intelligent haunting, does not directly involve a spiritual entity aware of the living world and interacting with or responding to it.'

Though I was still hesitant to admit it to myself, this sounded awfully similar to what I had seen in the bakery. I checked the notes I had taken on the night I crept down to the toilet and spied on the Moreaus. It all added up. When I watched the man, or the image of a man, working at the table alongside Manu, I noticed that he wasn't actually handling any dough. He seemed to be performing the movements of a baker kneading dough, but he wasn't actually connecting with anything around him. I felt a cold hand of fear grip my stomach as I remembered the image of that man, with the phantom glow lighting up his skin and his old-fashioned clothes marking him out as being from another time. Could it have been possible? There was only one thing for it now – I had to confront Mme Moreau.

Chapter 16

The following evening, as though he had sensed my intention, Manu left a key on the mat outside my door. It was an old heavy key and I knew exactly which door it would fit. I set my alarm for three a.m., so I would have time to get into the basement before Mme Moreau. There was some trepidation on my part, not least at the thought of being in the same room with a ghost, but as to how Mme Moreau would react. I realised that my predecessor Maria must have found out about the unsettling secret in the basement and high-tailed it out of there. Geoff had told me that she was also English and left without saying anything to anyone. Not that I blamed her – it's not exactly what you'd expect to find in a quaint little French *boulangerie*. Besides, who would have believed such a story? Unless, like me, they saw it with their own two eyes. I now firmly believed that fate or destiny had brought me here at this mid-point in my life, following my mother's passing. I didn't want to run away without facing the mystery of this place and its past.

I crept downstairs as quietly as I could. I felt more awake than I had done in a very long time, considering that all about me was darkness. Once I reached the kitchenette, I turned on the light and wiggled the key into the lock of the little door leading to the basement. The sound of my heart beating in my ears would have woken the dead, I thought, and immediately hoped that wasn't true. 'What are you doing Edie?' I asked myself, coldly resigned to the fact that there was no turning back now. I turned the key and heard the click. As the little door creaked open, a blast of cold air hit me in the face. I felt my knees trembling and threatening to give way. I would have reconsidered the whole thing then and there, but I heard noises coming from upstairs, which only meant one thing. Mme Moreau was up and would shortly come down to the basement herself. I steadied myself and took the torch from my dressing gown pocket. Closing the door behind me, I stepped carefully down the small staircase to the basement.

Manu had left a note with the key, advising me where to position myself. Seeing the bakery from the vantage point of the bathroom offered me some kind of safety, but being in the actual room was far too close for comfort. I found the bags of flour that Manu had said to hide behind and took up my position. From there I had a clear view of the great ovens that produced Moreau's famously crusty bread and I could see the large troughs they used for mixing the dough too, which had been obscured from my little spy hole in the toilet. Old wooden shelves lined the walls and were stacked with rose gold pots and loaf tins. A large weighing scale sat at the other end of the room, where the dough was cut and rolled before baking.

I sat in complete silence, with every hair on my body alert. Something lightly brushed against my ankle and I instinctively shrieked with terror. I clasped my hand over my mouth and hoped to God I wasn't being attacked by a zombie. On closer inspection, I saw that the culprit was the belt of my robe coming loose and didn't know whether to feel relieved or embarrassed.

All of a sudden, I heard the key turn in the lock and realised that Mme Moreau and her grandson were on their way, which meant that 'he' was surely on his way too. I took whatever breadcrumbs of courage I had left in my hands and tried to steady my breathing. I remembered the information I had read about residual hauntings and tried to remind myself that it was essentially a film on re-run, nothing more. Wordlessly, the two of them entered the bakery, although I could see

Manu's eyes darting about for me. If he couldn't see me, then I knew I had hidden myself well. Perhaps he thought I had chickened out. There wasn't much time for him to consider this, as straight away he began loading the oven with wood from a pile in the opposite corner of the room. That was when I noticed the door, which must have led to the street at some point, but I would have to investigate that later.

As the wood began to crackle and spark, the room filled with the low light from the fire and Manu set about emptying large quantities of flour into one of the troughs. Mme Moreau moved about stiffly, preparing the additional ingredients Manu would need. After a thorough mixing of the yeast and the water, which he didn't bother to measure, he scraped the dough together and transferred it to the worktop. The smell of the flour and the sweet/sour yeast made me feel at home and I almost forgot the reason I was there. Watching him expertly throw the flour over the surface, I found myself becoming lost in the process, until the flickering began and the atmosphere in the room changed completely. It felt as though there was an electric charge running through the air and then, from nowhere, he appeared. I jolted from the shock of seeing him at close quarters and almost knocked over the bag of flour that concealed my presence. However, no one seemed to hear me or notice, as they in turn jumped at his sudden apparition, despite the fact they were expecting him. What Mme Moreau said next shocked me even further.

"*Bonjour Papa.*"

I was frozen to the spot. This was no random haunting; I was watching the ghost of Monsieur Moreau. I had to stuff the belt of my robe into my mouth to ensure I wouldn't scream. M Moreau, or rather his ghost, seemed completely oblivious to the presence of his daughter and great-grandson, instead focusing intensely on his work. He moved about, not like a regular person, but just as the website had said. It was like watching an old, scratchy movie, where at one point the light around him would glow and the next almost fade completely. He reached for objects but never quite connected with them. He seemed unwilling or unable to interact with Manu, who watched his grandfather carefully and did his best to emulate his technique. It was startling and amazing to watch. They both flicked out their wrists to spread the flour on the board, then began the process of kneading and adding various ingredients along the way. While the breads were set aside to prove, Manu continued to shadow M Moreau as he placed a pot of steaming water in the oven and using a long wooden paddle, placed the round breads at the very back and closed the door. The only conversation was between Mme Moreau and Manu, surprisingly ordinary things like 'make sure the temperature of the water is right for the dough' and 'the baguettes are ready for the oven now'. Somehow, this bizarre and unique set-up had become normal for them. Mme Moreau watched her father lovingly, but was careful not to get too close.

This carried on for over two hours, by which stage my entire body was aching from crouching behind the large bags of flour on a cold floor. It was then I heard Mme Moreau suggest that she start taking the cooked breads upstairs and get ready to open the shop. I knew the moment of truth had arrived and I had to make my presence known. I didn't want to frighten them by popping up out of nowhere, but considered that if they had spent the morning sharing their kitchen with a ghost, my presence shouldn't come as that much of a shock.

"Good morning, Mme Moreau," was all I could say, as I stumbled out from behind my hiding place. She staggered and thankfully Manu grabbed onto her arm to offer her support.

"*Mais, qu'est ce que….* You!" she shouted at me with a mix of fury and guilt at being found out.

Just as he had appeared, M Moreau's image vanished from the scene and neither of us said anything for a while. Manu was the bravest among us and ushered his grandmother to a stool.

"*Elle veut nous aider*," he assured her gently.

"He's right" I added, "I do want to help, if I can," I said. I wasn't quite sure what I was signing up to, or why Manu thought I could possibly help them, but I would have said anything at that point, for Mme Moreau looked so pale and shaky, I feared for her health. I went and fetched her a glass of water, which she gulped in one go. She ordered Manu to get the bread ready for the shop and to prepare his deliveries and assuaged his worries with a persuasive nod of the head that she would be all right. I wasn't sure if the same could be said for me. I was still shivering myself and I wasn't sure if it was the cold or the shock. She must have sensed this, so she heaved herself off the stool and bade me to follow her. We climbed the stairs and with another nod of encouragement to Manu as we passed through the shop, we climbed the next set of stairs to her apartment. I had never seen past her front door up till now and the significance of bringing me into her home was not lost on me. It was, like my own apartment, small and functional, but hers was extremely cosy and homely. It was carpeted and had frilly drapes that hung from the long windows overlooking the street. Her fireplace was home to lots of old photographs of the bakery and what I assumed to be her mother. Then I saw M Moreau in another frame and recognised him instantly. The thick moustache and neatly gelled back hair were unmistakable.

"*Assieds-toi*," she said, pointing to one of two wing-backed chairs arranged in front of the fire. I was glad of the heat and rubbed my hands in front of the low embers. Mme Moreau boiled some water on the cooker and prepared a pot of strong coffee for us both. She placed the cups on a little side table and sat down in the chair opposite me.

"I underestimated you Édith," she said, with a look of approval on her face.

And there it was - approval. My drug of choice. All I ever wanted was the approval of those around me. Yet now that I had finally won this taciturn woman over, I no longer cared what she thought of me, for I was so angry with her.

"Was this some sort of test? I thought you hired me to become the shop manager, not a ghostbuster!" I knew I was being facetious, but hysteria will do that to a woman.

"*Mais non*, of course not," she argued.

"Oh really? What about Maria then? Yes, I've heard about your last employee," I said, seeing her surprise. "Is that why you insist on hiring foreigners, so we can't tell anyone what's going on here?"

"Partly, yes."

I had expected some sort of argument, for her to tell me I'd got the wrong end of the stick.

"Oh, so you're admitting it?" I could feel the blood rising to my cheeks with rage.

"*Édith, écoute-moi,* I was not trying to fool you or test you as you say. *Mais*, I cannot risk anyone here finding out. They will think we are…" at this stage she tapped her index finger against her temple and whistled like a cuckoo.

"Well it's not fair, hiring people to work here and not telling them the truth," I said, taking a sip of coffee that was thankfully good and hot.

"Would you have taken the job if I had told you the truth?"

114

I left the question hanging in mid-air. Of course the answer was no, but moreover, how could you tell anyone that you had a ghost in your basement without sounding like a lunatic.

"We cannot talk for long now," she said, checking her watch, "but I promise, I will explain you everything tonight."

I regarded her carefully and wondered how we were supposed to carry on as normal for the day in the shop. Then it became clear to me that she and Manu had done exactly that, for years. It was their reality.

"You have known for some time, yet you are still here," she said sincerely. "Why did you not leave us?"

"I'm not sure" I answered honestly, "The truth is, I came here to get away from my own problems and despite, well, this," I gestured at the floor below us, "I kind of like it here. It's going to sound strange, but there's something about the place that has given me back my appetite for life, you know?" I wrinkled my nose with a half-hearted smile. I hadn't really understood how true it was until that moment.

"Well, I am glad you stay," she said, patting my knee. "*Maintenant*, we must work!" she announced and something in her practicality made me put aside my misgivings. As I rose up out of my chair and prepared to follow her downstairs, she turned and gave me one of her withering looks.

"What now?" I asked impatiently.

"Oh nothing, perhaps this is your new uniform, *hein*?" she replied, eyeing me up and down.

That's when I realised that I was still in my dressing gown.

"Hang on, did you just make a joke?" I said, smiling triumphantly. She walked away, but we both knew I had cracked her hard shell. Edith one, France nil.

Chapter 17

Commerce always comes first for a sole trader and Mme Moreau was no different. She interacted with her customers as usual from her perch behind the counter, while I carried out my work in a daze. Just before lunch, Geoff popped by for a 'cheeky éclair' as he put it and I was never so happy to see anyone in my life.

"How is my favourite customer today?" I asked while wiping down his table. Mme Moreau must have wondered whether or not I was going to share her eerie secret with an outsider, but if she was concerned, she did not show it. Her face was an inscrutable mask.

"How's Ruby and the doggies?" I asked, craving a normal conversation after the extraordinary events of the morning.

"Little's having his nails clipped and Large has got the runs. It's not been pretty. Ruby's gone in for a grooming!"

"What?" I said, hardly catching the joke. "Oh, right, very funny."

"What's up Irish?"

"Me? Oh you know, just tired" I said.

"Retail therapy," he said, licking his fingers. "Whenever my Ruby is out of sorts, she swears by retail therapy. I always say that's fine, as long as you don't arrive home with silly outfits for the dogs. Not under my roof, I said not under my roof!" he ranted.

"You know what, that might not be such a bad idea" I said, untying my apron. "I might just take an early lunch and see if I can't shop my way into a better mood."

Instead of asking, I simply told Mme Moreau that I was leaving and walked out into the watery sunshine. I walked and walked from one end of the town to the other, searching for some unknown object that might make everything seem normal again. Seeing M Moreau that morning brought up some unwelcome thoughts about death and the afterlife. To think I had come to France to get away from all of that, only to end up coming face to face with a real live, or dead, ghost. Where was his soul after all? Trapped in some kind of limbo? I wasn't sure if I believed in heaven, but I wanted to believe that my mother was happy, wherever she was. Shop windows held nothing but my own bemused reflection and so I kept walking. I ended up walking along by the river, where I had sat with Hugo on that one wonderful night. I flumped down on our bench and looked out across the city.

Despite my frustration at being lied to, I couldn't help but wonder what it must feel like for Mme Moreau to see her father like that, night after night. I couldn't imagine seeing my mother in that way; not as herself but as an echo of herself. On the one hand, it would be so wonderful to see her again, but to not be able to touch her or speak to her? I realised that it would be a kind of breath-taking torture. I wasn't really sure if I could deal with it. I mean, I was still in the process of grieving myself. Without thinking about it, I called my Dad.

"How are ya getting on Edie?" he greeted me, full of the joys. I could feel the tears stinging my eyes and tried desperately to hold onto them. I was holding tightly onto the bench, watching the river rushing by in front of me.

"I miss her so much Dad," was all I could say, as the tears came out in torrents. He said nothing for a while, but from the sounds he made, I felt he was crying too.

"Do you want to come home love?" he asked eventually, his voice hoarse.

"Yes," I said, snivelling like a little girl who just wanted her father to make everything go away. "But, I think they need me here," I said, which was a revelation. I remembered how Manu had said I would help them and it was then that I realised, despite their air of nonchalance in the bakery that morning, they were struggling somehow.

"They're lucky to have you Edie, you know that," he said with paternal pride.

"You know what? You're right!" I said, as though suddenly understanding my position in the world. Maybe it wasn't my destiny to become a chart topping singer or a celebrity chef, or even a Stepford wife with 2.3 children and a dog. But I had the ability to impact on peoples' lives, if only in a small way, just by being myself – and that was enough. I began walking back towards my street, but stopped in front of a window with a mannequin wearing a red prom-style dress with a halter neck. It was over the top, frivolous and on sale. I bought it without even trying it on and realised that Geoff's wife Ruby was right; shopping could cure all ills.

***

That evening, Mme Moreau had me round for dinner. It had begun snowing outside and the temperature had dropped rapidly, so her cosy apartment was a welcome refuge. She had prepared a delicious rabbit stew with lots of comforting root vegetables.

"*Manu ne mange pas avec nous*?" I asked, when I noticed he was not at table.

"*Il sort avec ses amis*," she said. "Your French is improving."

"*Merci*, I've always wanted to speak fluent French – that's why I came here really," I said, enjoying the opportunity to open up to this woman who had kept me at arm's length since I arrived. She dished out our meal from a china terrine onto pretty plates with blue flowers, while I poured the wine. We ate in companionable silence for a time, with only the sound of the ticking clock and the sparking logs in the background. As I mopped up the sauce with my bread, we spoke about ordinary things like the weather and some of the interesting characters that came into the shop. She had prepared a delicious *tarte tatin* with caramelised apples in cinnamon and despite my full stomach, I cleaned the bowl. After we had cleared away the dishes, we moved to the chairs beside the fire once again and I knew it was time to discuss the elephant in the room.

"You didn't really need a manager for the shop who spoke English, did you?" I said, suddenly understanding the motivation behind the job being advertised abroad. "You didn't want anyone from around here finding out about your father, or risk them telling anyone."

"I never want to upset or frighten anyone, but yes, it was easier to keep the secret that way. It has been difficult – trying to hide this. That is why we use the tunnel for the deliveries, that way I can avoid anyone coming into the basement," she explained, solving the other mystery that had me baffled. "When my daughter was alive, I did not need any help from the outside. But now, my arthritis is bad and Manu must go to school.." she shrugged.

"I'm sorry, I had no idea your daughter had passed away," I said genuinely.

Her eyes glistened as she said, "No parent should see their child go before them." She searched for a tissue in the pocket of her house coat and wiped her eyes.

"I'm so sorry," I said again, the words sounding so small and insignificant. Now I understood what it was like for my family and friends when they felt so helpless.

"It was a car accident. 12 years ago. She and her husband were travelling south to Spain, to visit his family. Little Manu, he was sleeping in the rear seat."

It was visibly distressing for her to talk about it, so I stopped her with my hand on her arm and told her it was okay, she didn't have to explain.

"I lost my mother – I know it's hard to talk about it sometimes," I said in solidarity. Her face was the picture of empathy; such was the softness of her large brown eyes as she placed her hand on mine.

"*C'est dur la vie, hein*?"

In the silence that followed, I understood how my first impressions of Mme Moreau were completely wrong. I interpreted her frosty demeanour as an undesirable personality trait, when in actual fact; she was merely doing her best to protect her family and her own peace of mind. She stood up and went to a tall mahogany dresser and took a photo album out of one of the cupboards. Sitting back down beside me, she showed me pictures of her daughter from childhood right up until before she died.

"She would be just a year or two older than you," she told me in a soft voice.

"Does Manu remember them at all?" I asked, but she just shook her head, saying he was only a baby then.

"He's such a bright young man, and a credit to you."

"*Comment*?" she said, unfamiliar with the term.

"You have brought him up extremely well," I said. Then a thought struck me. "Your daughter?"

"*Gabrielle, oui*?"

"Did she see your father too?" I asked.

"But of course, it was she who was learning the old methods from him - she was to take over the *boulangerie*. Not that it matters now," she added.

120

"Why do you say that? Manu is doing a good job, isn't he? My father used to work as a patissière at home in Ireland, so I know a thing or two about baking and Manu really has the flair for it."

"Ah yes, I remember this in your application. Manu said it could be useful," she smiled proudly at her grandson's foresight.

"Oh I see, so it's Manu I should thank for giving me the job?" I said smiling too.

"Indeed, but as I am sure you know, small bakeries are not so profitable anymore. People are buying those *moche*, how you say, horrible sliced breads in the supermarket because they are cheaper and with all those preserves that keep it from going stale for days and days, ugh!"

"I suppose, there is a recession on and people are just trying to save money."

"*Exactement*, so they do not buy their fresh bread and croissants everyday. Things are becoming very difficult for us here, I don't know what future there is." She stared into the fire and for the first time since I had known her, she looked tired. I didn't want to press her about the small issue of a ghost in the basement, but I couldn't hide my curiosity either.

"So, what about your father?" I asked in as sensitive a tone as possible.

"Ah yes, well, you deserve to know the truth now Edith and I will tell it to you. *Mais*, I have to start at the very beginning".

Chapter 18

My earliest memories are sitting around a campfire, watching my mother dance. She wore *une robe*, a beautiful dress with flowers in yellow and red that twirled with her body. My grandmother and all the other women clapped, while one of the men played his guitar and my mother tapped her feet on the dusty earth. Her name was Mirela, in Romani language it means 'to admire', which was right because everyone who saw her admired her. I remember the warmth of our brightly painted caravane and the sounds when the camp stirred at first light, with pots and pans rattling and children laughing.

I know that these are the romantic notions of a child. I mean, what child would not enjoy the freedom of a nomadic life? You are not expected to go to school and you live close with all your family, so there is always something to do and someone to play with. It is life from a child's perspective, but even then I could see the hardship for my parents. Roma were very disliked by many of the locals and we were chased from one campsite to the next, *très souvent*. My family were 'Manouche', a small group of Roma who came to France from Eastern Europe. We were so very poor, but we were a proud people and did what we could to make a living. My father traded in horses and he worked sometimes training them in the stables of the rich. He spoke many languages and in fact it was he who taught me to speak English. We learned how to survive and use our skills to make a living on the edges of society. But there was always uncertainty and our caravans were always on the move.

My memories of that time have become golden; they are so precious to me. When I think of my mother back then, all I remember are the sparks from the fire lighting up the sky and how her body resembled the dancing flames, swaying and diving and lulling us all into a trance. She was *très belle*, with long black hair braided down her back, like one of my father's stallions. They said she had the '*duende*'; that she danced with passion and fire in her soul and people would come from all around to see her.

Things began to change in France and I could often hear the adults talking about the war. I did not fully understand what a war was, but I knew that people were frightened. When France signed the Armistice with the Nazis in 1940, I was eight years old. I thought I knew what hardship was, but life was to become much more difficult with the occupation. The Germans made the French pay for the occupation and the prices for everyday goods inflated. People were already poor, but now there were no jobs, so people were trying to survive on very little. With the curfews and the Vichy Regime punishing anyone who resisted the rules, life in France became *intolérable*. But the worst was yet to come.

For some time, we had heard the rumours of German labour camps. Hitler's regime had begun the rounding up of minority groups considered 'racially inferior'. Jews, Poles, Roma, homosexuals and people with disabilities were being sent to labour camps or shot, to protect the Aryan race. Of course, my family did not tell me this at the time, but I remember hearing about a crazy man in Germany who wanted to take over the world. It did not seem real to me. Not until my father disappeared.

We were staying in a camp just east of Paris when a small troop of German soldiers pulled up in their army jeeps. They said the men were needed for work and that we would all be moved to a town in the north I had never heard of, called Compiègne. The men had to leave with them *immédiatement,* and the women and children were to take a train. I remember feeling nervous and scared, but that my mother reassured me all would be well. She said that papa was a good worker and that was why he was being asked to go in such a hurry. He held me fiercely in his arms and told me to be good for my mother. I never saw him again.

There was some excitement getting on the train, because it was my first time and despite the confusion, I was eager to get moving. I remember how quickly the landscape moved past, not like our caravan and the old horse that clip-clopped along the lanes. It was no time at all before we pulled into the station and I noticed German guards all around. I did not know why at the time, but my mother yanked me up out of my seat and pulled me behind her towards the exit *en vitesse*. She must have spotted him as we pulled in and saw her chance. An ordinary man, dressed in an overcoat with a white apron underneath, stood on the platform holding a large basket of baguettes. I had no idea what she was doing, or how she seemed to know this man, but as soon as we alighted from the train she ran to him and embraced him, rather vigorously and spoke to him in what I thought was a very posh accent.

"*Chéri*, you've come to greet us off the train!" she said, kissing his face. *Il y avait un regard*, a look that passed between them then that I couldn't explain. A pause that seemed to last just a second too long. One of the officers approached and was about to say something, when Monsieur Moreau put down the basket and put his arms around us both.

"Welcome home my darlings, how I've missed you!"

***

124

Mme Moreau put some more wood logs on the fire and fetched two glasses and a bottle of brandy. I was enraptured by her story and stunned by its stark realities.

"So, he saved you from the concentration camps?" I said, hardly believing the dramatic childhood traumas she must have witnessed.

"For a time, yes. Maman explained to me that, while my father was away, M Moreau or Charles, would be like *mon oncle*. But in public, I was to call him 'Papa'. She said it would not be like betraying Papa, because he wanted me to be safe and looked after until he returned. I'm not sure if she believed he would come back, or if that was just for my benefit. My young eyes never saw any artifice. We lived quietly in this apartment for many months. M Moreau was a kind, good-natured man. I always remember his funny moustache, curling at the ends and his great mess of dark hair. As long as he was working in his bakery, he was happy. Kneading dough, rolling pastry and turning the hot, crusty bread out of the oven was his passion.

"Bread is a living thing" he used to tell me. "If you put your heart into the dough, you'll spread happiness to all who eat your bread!" His *enthousiasme* was contagious and I spent many happy hours working with him in the kitchen. He encouraged my love of English also, and borrowed many books for me from the library. M Moreau was a very well respected man in the community and when he took us in, most of the locals admired his *générosité*. Most of them. As always, our presence in a town divided opinion and one day, when I was in the basement playing with some dough and making little animal shapes, I heard shouting upstairs in the shop. I climbed the stairs and peered through the doorway. I recognised the uniforms instantly and to my horror, I saw two soldiers holding my mother. She looked at me frantically, then composed herself and winked. I knew what that meant – disappear. In the basement, there is a doorway that leads onto an old underground tunnel that runs all the way to an opening by the river. It was how they delivered the flour in the old days, when the boats sailed down from the mill, but it hadn't been used for years. M Moreau had told us that if anything ever happened, we could escape from the building through the tunnel. Like frightened prey, I ran through the darkness and never looked back. As soon as I reached the opening, I hid in the thicket along the riverbank until it grew dark. I was sure no one had followed me, as I kept an eye on the opening, hoping against hope that my mother would emerge and take me back with her. But no one came.

After hours of shivering with the cold, I crept back into the pitch blackness of the tunnel and arrived back to find M Moreau in the basement, sobbing *comme un enfant*. When he heard my footsteps behind him, he turned and took me to his breast in pure elation. He kissed my head and my face and cried for joy at my return. But I stood limp in his arms.

"Where is Maman?" I asked, though I knew the answer.

"I tried to stop them," he explained. "And I will do all I can to get her back," he promised. "But from now on, you must stay out of sight, Geneviève."

And so that was my life, until the war ended. I stayed in hiding at the top of the house, in your little apartment during the day, and worked with M Moreau in the bakery at night."

"My God, I don't know what to say," I said after some time had passed.

"There is nothing to be said. War, genocide, it pushes human beings to do ugly things. But I found that it also brought about the most beautiful kind of humanity. M Moreau protected me with his life. I was just a young girl, someone he didn't even know and yet he became my father."

126

"Geoff, the English guy who comes here? He took me to the Armistice Memorial in the forest," I said, recalling his commitment to remembering the lives lost during that terrible time in history.

"There was a camp there. That is where they were taking us – Royallieu-Compiègne. My mother used her wits that day at the train station and we were lucky to escape. But I found out later that is where they took her. It was an internment and deportation camp. Between 1942 and 1944 they deported 40,000 people from there to Auschwitz".

"How did you survive? I mean, how did you carry on after that?" I asked, cognisant of my own struggles after my mother's death, which in contrast to this, was peaceful and dignified.

"M Moreau," she said simply. "He saved me in every way. He gave me an appetite for life again. When the war ended, I began working in the *boulangerie* and learned to bake at his side. We spent every day together, kneading, folding and baking the stuff of life."

"Do you think that's why he's remained?" I said, recalling my research online and the inability of some spirits to let go.

"I don't care to know why. He said he would always be here for me. Even in death he stays true to his promise. But it will not last much longer," she said.

"What do you mean?"

"It used to be that he was here all the time, day and night I could see him. Now, he stays for just one or two hours, that's it. It will all end soon." She sipped her brandy and let her gaze fall onto the dancing flames of the fire.

I guessed that these residual hauntings couldn't go on indefinitely, but it seemed almost cruel to think of Mme Moreau and Manu carrying on without his reassuring presence. "But what about Manu? He is going to take over some day, isn't he? I mean, he is learning from the master, I could see that."

Mme Moreau's eyes shone with pride, then clouded with uneasiness once again. "We are being forced to sell Édith," she sighed, "I have to sell the *boulangerie*."

"I don't believe it, after everything you've told me? It's impossible!" I had not expected to hear that and couldn't hide my shock.

"You think I want this?" she shouted, her voice full of emotion. She reached to the mantelpiece and took a letter down. It was from the bank and while it was written in formal language, I could guess what the contents were. The Moreaus were in debt and the bank wanted them to sell. A howling wind had picked up outside and the snow whirled in circles outside the window. Mme Moreau got up with difficulty to close them, her arthritis clearly paining her.

"I've worked hard every day of my life to keep our home," she said, looking around the apartment she had shared for so long with M Moreau. "But when Gabrielle died, there was only me left to take care of Manu. The bills kept coming in, books for his school, clothes, food and the costs of running the *boulangerie*. I had to borrow a, how you say, *hypothèque* on our home and I can no longer make the payments."

"Oh, I see," I said, looking down into my lap, "a mortgage".

"They came last month, the men in their suits with pale faces and avarice eyes. It would seem there is a buyer, eager to develop the building into a boutique hotel."

"What? But that's ridiculous; the bakery has been here for years, hasn't it?"

"Since 1849, the Moreaus have been baking their bread here," she said, distraught at the thought of being the one to lose the tradition that had been kept in the family for generations.

"Surely the town council wouldn't allow it," I argued, "I mean this has got to be a listed building."

"*Mais c'est ça le problème*, it's expensive to keep up the building and the developers have promised the council that they wish the exterior to remain the same, but that they will restore the interiors to preserve the building for years to come. These historic societies are very strict about these things, *sensibilité* to the building's origins, but they don't care who is paying for it. The bank believes a hotel will be more profitable, so they are supporting the deal. The developers have promised the council increased tourist numbers with an historical hotel. I don't see what I can do."

"But Manu, I can see that baking is his passion. What does he think?"

"Ah yes, he learns well from Papa. But he is just a child. I wanted to give him the home M Moreau gave to me after my parents died. But now we will lose everything – even him."

That was when she finally broke down. The pressure of keeping everything together must have been enormous. I knelt down beside her and put my arm around her shoulders while she cried into her tissue. Manu's words in the basement that morning came back to me; 'Maybe she can help'. What on earth did he think I could do? Well, I couldn't make things any worse, that was for sure. I would have to think of something.

Chapter 19

Another postcard arrived the following morning. This one was an aerial shot of the market square, with colourful tarpaulins covering the maze of stalls selling their wares in Place du Capitole. On the back, a simple message:

I'll be back in Compiègne next week,

Hope to see you Edie.

Hugo x

My stomach performed a back flip that left me unsure as to whether I was excited or terrified, or both. If I was being honest, I had pushed any thoughts of him to the back of my mind since my evening with Mme Moreau. Her tragic story had affected me deeply and raised a lot of issues surrounding my own mother's passing. I now found myself feeling unutterably grateful for the time we had together, all those close hours sharing each other's likes and dislikes, singing songs and eating cake. I realised how privileged we all were as a family to have shared such a wonderful life together and even when I thought of her lying on her deathbed, I could no longer experience the grief of loss without it being tempered by gratitude for having lived with my mother well into my thirties. I knew Mme Moreau's story held far more pain and terror than she had revealed. Not only had she lost her parents, but she had lost her culture as well. She grew up as a French girl, daughter to the local baker and was never again to speak about her Roma heritage.

I didn't want to keep bombarding her with questions of the past, so I took myself off to the Internet café again later that week and did some research of my own. The 'Porajmos' as some called it, or the Romani Holocaust was responsible for the near annihilation of the Roma population in Europe, killing hundreds of thousands of people. I was completely unaware of this aspect of World War II, as I was under the impression that the Nuremberg Law referred only to the Jewish community. Just as Mme Moreau had said, I discovered that there had been an internment camp in Compiègne, used for members of the resistance as well as Roma and Jews, before sending them on to camps such as Auschwitz. It made for horrifying reading, but to know someone who had lived through that time and was now about to lose everything she had fought for, to some greedy developers? Well I simply couldn't let that happen.

***

"I've got to find a USP, you know?" I said to my Dad on the phone later that night.

"A what now?" he said, confused.

"A unique selling point! Come on Dad, get with the program. I just thought, with all your expertise, you might be able to think of something that would get the business going again and attract new customers," I explained. We had already discussed the shift from baguettes to supermarket sliced pans and the ailing European economy.

"Loyalty cards are always a nice incentive for the regulars," he began, clearly happy to be asked for his opinion.

"Yes, I was thinking that too," I agreed, jotting down bullet points in my notebook.

"And, you did say it's a bit of a touristy place, yeah?"

"Yes, lots of Brits and people come here from Paris at the weekends too," I said.

"Let's see, right well it is France," he began.

"Yes, we've established that," I sighed with impatience, staring at the discoloured ceiling overhead.

"So, there's no point in competing with the finer Pâtisseries," he continued.

"No, I suppose not."

"Well then, I think the best you can do in the short term is to bring a bit of fun to the shop front window – entice the customers in you know. So I'd say cupcakes. Your only man."

"Huh?" I felt a bit deflated that this was his big plan for saving the bakery. "Aren't cupcakes a bit, well, passé?"

"Ooh, you've got all the lingo now, haven't you? But tell me Miss know-it-all, have you ever seen macaroon cupcakes anywhere else in Compiègne?" he asked.

I'd never even heard of macaroon cupcakes.

"Um, no, actually but I don't really think Moreaus is a cupcake kind of place," I said uncertainly.

"Well macaroon cupcakes are all the rage in Paris now you know" he said, mimicking a teenage American girl, "oh yes, your old Da keeps up to date with the world of baking. It's a no-brainer, you'll earn a bigger return for minimal expenditure and you could even do those cake pops the kids love," he added. "What were the ones you used to make, white chocolate?"

My lips curled into a Cheshire grin at the thought of adding a bit of e-coloured sparkle to the Moreau's traditional window. "It could work, but oh, I dunno Dad, I only ever baked at home," I said, doubtfully.

"So did Nigella, and that didn't stop her, did it?"

"God you're obsessed with Nigella! Seriously though, you think I could do it?" I asked.

"Do I think you can save a business in debt and keep a roof over your boss's head? I don't know Edie. But do I think you can get more punters in the door with gimmicky cakes? Definitely!" he boomed with the deep baritone voice that had always kept his sous-chefs on their toes. "She's lucky to have you on her side and I've never known a man, woman or child that could pass up one of your cake pops!"

That was all the validation I needed.

"Thanks Dad and you're right; it's a start. And in the meantime, we'll try to come up with some sort of long-term business plan she can take to the bank."

"That's my girl," he said. "You never give up. Those frogs won't know what hit them!"

***

The next day, I asked Mme Moreau and Manu to have lunch with me in the shop when we closed. It felt quite nice, the three of us sitting together. Mme Moreau had prepared a tasty chicken liver pate and served it with a green salad and of course, sourdough bread. Manu was visibly more relaxed than I had ever seen him and he talked animatedly about the day he would finish completely with school and work full time in the bakery.

"Not until you complete your *baccelauréat*!" Mme Moreau rhymed off, as if this was an habitual argument they had. Having heard about her own lack of formal education, I could understand her vehemence, but Manu was obviously keen to become the next M Moreau.

"Right, order - I call order!" I shouted to get their attention. "I've been trying to think of ways we can drum up more business and after talking to my Dad, we were thinking of maybe targeting the tourists with things like cupcakes and cake pops?"

I half expected tumbleweed to blow through the shop, such was their lack of enthusiasm.

"I don't know how to make these cake-hops?" Manu answered eventually.

"Well that's just it, I'll be making them!"

Another drawn out silence followed.

"Maybe it's better if I show you." Luckily, I had prepared some of my infamous 'French toast' cupcakes with maple syrup butter cream, and a nutmeg flavoured cake. A miniature cinnamon infused macaroon sat jauntily atop the frosting, like a little confectionary hat. I could see in their eyes that I had gone up in their estimations and when I presented a basket full of decorated white chocolate cake pops poking out on little sticks, I knew I had won them over.

"We mightn't become millionaires overnight, but I think if we stick these in the window, we might bring in some new customers," I explained, as they munched their way through my samples.

"I had no idea you could bake like this Edith," Mme Moreau marvelled. "Mmm, they are very sweet," she noted with pursed lips.

"I like them," Manu decided, and seeing as he was my target demographic, the decision was made. I was now part of the Moreau baking team.

I set to work the very next day, and began my baking in the afternoons when we were quiet. Manu had assured me that there would be no-one or nothing keeping me company in the basement at that hour, which gave me some modicum of comfort. Despite my efforts to understand M Moreau's residual haunting of the bakery, it didn't make it any less unnerving to be down there. I always brought my radio with me and to my surprise, I found myself singing along to some of the songs that were in the charts. Over time I noticed myself picking up vocabulary by osmosis and the realisation made me smile. Sometimes if you just let things happen, rather than trying to force them, they come easier.

I enjoyed baking again. Down in the basement, I was free to make as much mess as I liked and so I sent clouds of flour puffing towards the ceiling as I tried to get the hang of the old weighing scales. There was a sort of alchemy to it; combine flour, eggs, butter and sugar, and you've got the basis for the most sublime cakes whose only flavour limit is your own imagination. I made peanut butter ones, red velvet dark chocolate ones and vanilla white chocolate ones. I felt like the Willy Wonka of cupcakes and relished my new role in the baking team.

When Manu finished school in the afternoon, he would come down and make a good stab at eating all of my frosting.

"I tell the other kids at school about your cakes, so maybe they will stop by," he said, licking his fingers.

"That's great Manu, let's hope we have something to offer them when they arrive," I said, yanking the bowl away from him. "How are you getting on with our website?"

"We are live tomorrow and already on Facebook, we 'ave 150 likes!"

Mme Moreau looked blankly at us both.

"I knew you would help us," he said later, in a rare moment of openness and out of Mme Moreau's earshot.

"How did you know that?" I said, sprinkling the cupcakes with cinnamon sugar.

"Because you are alone," he replied simply.

"Eh, that's not really a compliment Manu," I stuttered, "I thought you were going to say something like, 'You have kind eyes'."

"Well, no I mean of course you do," he explained, backtracking, "but you see, if you were marry with childrens, they would be for you a priority, right? Not this old place, not

us. We're lucky that no-one else found you before we did."
He was happy with this cockeyed explanation.

"So I guess what you're trying to say is, it's lucky I haven't
been snapped up?" I said, squinting at him.

"*C'est ça, oui!*"

It was at that point I decided to give him a butter cream face
mask.

***

Manu's little PR trick paid off, and that afternoon the
boulangerie was crammed with students from the local *lycée*,
all curious to try out *les gateaux irlandaises*. It was a roaring
success and Mme Moreau was visibly pleased to see such a
young clientele livening up the place. Still, I knew we would
have to keep up the momentum if this was going to make any
impact on the business plan for the bank. The following
morning I went to the printers to pick up our new loyalty
cards, offering a free croissant when you bought five, or a free
baguette. They were a bit gimmicky, but at least it showed the
boulangerie's customers that we were moving with the times
and planning to stick around.

"I take it this is your input," Geoff remarked, when he and
Ruby stopped by for their weekly treat.

"Well you know you can't stand still in business," I said, not
entirely sure of what I meant.

"Ooh, I'd love to try one of your cupcakes," said Ruby
"they look delicious."

***

Everything was going according to plan, until he showed up.
It was Friday afternoon and I was in the kitchen, dipping my

cake pops into hundreds and thousands. I heard the little bell over the door ring, but took no notice of it until I heard Mme Moreau's tone of voice change from welcoming to downright hostile.

"You have no right to come in here," she said in English, which made me pop my head around the door.

I could hardly believe my eyes when I saw Hugo standing at the counter with another man, both of them sharply dressed and carrying briefcases. Seeing his face again filled me with sheer joy, but that soon faded when I heard him speak.

"We have been given permission by the bank and their estate agent to view the property Mme Moreau" he said in a clipped tone.

Then the man beside him stepped in. "You did receive my letter regarding our visit, Mme?"

That was when Mme Moreau broke into a tirade of abuse in French that I could hardly understand. It seemed I had been frozen to the spot while they argued, as I physically had to pull my feet from their entrenched position to go to her aid. I put my hand on her shoulder and guided her back to her stool, giving her a glass of water, despite her considerable efforts to ignore me. I turned back to the men.

"Edith," Hugo said, in a tone of voice that sounded almost rueful of my presence there.

"Hugo, what is this, what's going on? Why are you here – I thought you weren't coming till next week?"

He looked visibly uncomfortable as he fidgeted with his briefcase.

"Look, I'm sorry about this – I was hoping… well never mind." He produced a letter and asked if I would mind giving it to Mme Moreau once she had calmed down.

"I'm sorry, I really don't understand all of this," I said, glancing down at the envelope. I spotted a logo on the top right hand corner that looked familiar. Chadwick Holdings Inc. It took some time for the thoughts to form cohesively in my mind, but when I looked up at him, it suddenly became clear.

"Hugo Chadwick. Are you…?"

He turned his head to the side and sighed. "Will you step outside for a moment, I don't really want an audience," he said, looking around at the regulars who were all staring at us.

I agreed and closed the glass-panelled door behind me, aware that our audience were all but pressing their noses against the glass.

"My father was the CEO of Chadwick Holdings and now the board wants me to take over," he explained, as if that would somehow make things clearer to me.

"But they're some kind of property investors, right?" I asked and he nodded in confirmation. "I don't get it – I mean you told me you were a photographer?"

This time he just looked at the ground.

"Oh, I get it, that was just some stupid story to impress a girl in a bar." I turned away from him, feeling completely foolish.

He grabbed my arm and turned me around to face him again. "I am a photographer; it's just not what I do for a living, that's all. I didn't lie, Edith."

"No, you just weren't exactly forthcoming with the truth, were you?" I thought back to that night and his reaction when he walked me home. "That's why you acted so strange when I told you I was working here. You knew all about it, didn't you?"

"Of course I knew," he said angrily, trying to keep his voice down. "They're in debt up to their eyeballs," he said looking at the bakery "and my company, well we offer solutions."

"You mean you find businesses that are struggling and prey on them to satisfy your investors," I spat out my words. "And you know Mme Moreau and her son work 24/7 to keep this *boulangerie* alive. They are good people and they don't deserve to have their livelihood taken from under them by bullies like you!" I walked away completely enraged and slammed the door of the bakery in his face. Then I grabbed what I assumed to be the estate agent by the arm, struggled to open the door that had practically come off the hinges and slung him out into the street.

"And don't come back!" I shouted, slamming the door again for good measure. I felt so hurt and the look in Hugo's eyes made it worse. I couldn't tell if he was angry, guilty or relieved that our relationship had gone no further. But then the *boulangerie* broke into a spontaneous round of applause for me, led by Mme Moreau who had come out from behind the counter. I was shaking so much that I had to hold onto her for support, but on seeing a room full of outspoken, fearless French people applauding my courage, I had to smile.

Chapter 20

That night, I lay awake and turned the art of over-analysing into an Olympic sport. My ego was badly bruised, as was my heart. Still, I didn't feel as though I had the right to feel cheated; I mean we had only met that one night, but it was such a magical night and I knew he had felt it too. Then all those postcards; I mean why would he have sent them if it didn't mean something to him? I couldn't bear the thought of him being a part of the *boulangerie*'s demise. Perhaps if he knew the truth, he would see things differently; convince the board of Chadwick Holdings that this wasn't a good investment. But I knew I couldn't tell him – for starters he would probably think I was insane. Residual hauntings aren't exactly workable reasons for re-negotiating your mortgage. Although it didn't seem that the truth ranked high on his list of priorities, and that was what hurt the most. I didn't like being lied to, whatever the reason. Yet, there was a small part of me that wanted to believe he had his reasons. Still, that didn't change the fact that his company was going to take over the *boulangerie* and turn it into a boutique hotel. And if that happened, how could there be a future for us?

I awoke the next day with renewed vigour. I went down to the basement after the morning rush and began baking my cupcakes.

"*Merci pour hier,*" Mme Moreau said, poking her head around the door.

"Oh, it was nothing," I said, trying to hide my dilemma. "We'll find a solution to all of this, I promise." I knew I shouldn't have been making those kinds of promises, but in a strange way, I think she knew I was limited in what I could achieve. I was sure she must have tried all kinds of initiatives to try and fix things before I arrived, and it obviously hadn't worked. Then again, she wasn't the type of woman to ask for help and their particular circumstances meant that they had to be extremely secretive. I would have to do the asking on their behalf and began that very night.

It was a mild enough night for February, so I just wore a little black fur shrug over my new red dress. I knocked on Mme Moreau's door on my way out and her expression made me blush.

"*Très belle Édith*, you are beautiful in that dress! It is good to see you having fun. I'm afraid I didn't give you such a warm welcome when you arrived, but I was glad to hear Nicole had taken you under her wing," she said.

I realised nothing much could happen in Compiègne without Mme Moreau knowing about it. I remembered that Nicole's mother had only kind words for her too. This gave me a little hope, as I strutted down the street to meet Nicole at Nostalgie to watch Johnny and his band play. It was strange going back to the jazz club – I hadn't been there since the night I met Hugo and even though it was only a few weeks, it felt like a lifetime ago. It was a bittersweet feeling and I found myself half hoping that he would be there, although if he had been, I wasn't sure if I would hit him or kiss him. Nicole embraced me warmly as usual and oohed and aahed over my dress.

"How's little Max?" I asked, pulling out a chair for myself.

"Learning to play the guitar like his papa; it's quite the noise at 6 am!" she scowled.

I was practically bursting to tell her all about the goings on at the bakery, so as soon as I ordered some drinks, I spilled the beans about Hugo, Chadwick Holdings and the bakery's financial problems. I was so tempted to paint the full picture, haunting and all, but I was sworn to secrecy.

"*Conard*!" she seethed.

"Duck?" I was confused, but I suppose calling him a duck was as good as any other barnyard animal.

"No, not a duck," Nicole snorted, "a bastard!" she translated. "I hate those corporate pigs, they don't care about the little people."

I almost felt the need to defend Hugo then – it was awkward being so torn. I wanted to hate him too, but I just couldn't. Instead I tried to steer the conversation towards what we could do to help save the bakery.

"We'll think of something Edie, don't worry. We stick together in Compiègne," she winked, full of fighting spirit.

***

After another swinging session at the club, Johnny and Nicole walked me home. I invited them upstairs for a little brainstorming session and stuck on my Django CD for inspiration. As per usual, the electricity cut out, but I easily explained it away as faulty electrics in an old building. Just as we settled around the stove with a bottle of red wine and some snacks, a light knock at the door gave me a start. I was terrified that M Moreau would make some unplanned appearance and frighten them away. I walked hesitantly to the door and called out a tentative 'hello', but when I turned the knob, there stood Mme Moreau.

I was about to apologise for waking her or making too much noise, but she waved my apologies away. She asked if she might come in for a moment and of course we all welcomed her in.

"*C'est la musique,*" she said, "I heard you playing it again and I had to come upstairs to be sure; it is Django, non?"

I remembered her displeasure the last time I played his music, but this time she seemed to be smiling. Johnny, being

142

the expert among us in all things musical, confirmed that it was and this seemed to please her no end.

"I remember him as impulsive and wild. He was also something of a gambler, if I recall."

"You've met Django Reinhardt?" Johnny said, astounded.

"Met him? Why, he was my cousin," she laughed.

While Nicole and I were surprised, I thought Johnny was about to experience heart failure. His mouth hung open for a very long time and on seeing little or no response from us, Mme Moreau continued.

"He was a second cousin of my mother; he used to come and play in our camp sometimes. Everyone admired him, the way he learned to play the guitar again after that terrible fire in his caravan."

"Yes, his hand was crippled in a fire and he's famous for the unique style he created. He's like, the king of gypsy music. I mean, he's the reason I wanted to come to France and play guitar!" Johnny enthused, until a light cough from Nicole made him rephrase his words. "Well Django and Nicole of course, I came here for you hun," he smiled meekly.

Mme Moreau leaned against the sideboard and closed her eyes for a moment, lost in the music.

"He came to visit us here once, before my mother…," she broke off.

I looked at her and tried to let her know with a slight shake of my head that I hadn't told them the whole story.

"They've come to help," I said, hoping that she would trust them enough to tell them about her real parents. "I'll put on some coffee," I added, guessing that this would be a very long night.

Chapter 21

"When World War II broke out, the original quintet was on tour in the United Kingdom. Django returned to Paris at once, but Stephane Grappelli, the violinist, remained in England. He had word that my mother and I were living here with M Moreau and so he came by one evening to visit us. Some friends of M Moreau's heard that he was staying with us and came by to hear him play. You understand, at that time, there was very little to celebrate, so that evening stands out in my memory like it was yesterday," she said, with a fondness in her voice.

"I actually can't believe I'm hearing this!" said Johnny, for what seemed like the hundredth time. He was enthralled by Mme Moreau and her stories of 1940's France. But there was the harsh reality too that life for the Romani in Europe at that time was perilous and while her story had a happy ending, there was no escaping the cruelties suffered by her parents.

"Still today the Romani are treated as outcasts. When the industrial revolution began, our way of life and our craftsmanship was belittled. Our nomadic lifestyle no longer fitted in with the rest of society and the struggle continues even now."

We all reflected over the conversation, as Django Reinhardt played his own particular style of swinging guitar in the background. I started to feel as though we were outcasts too, in the eyes of Chadwick Holdings. Just a useless bakery with an apartment overhead, not making enough money to be considered financially viable.

"There's got to be a way to save the bakery," I said, bringing everyone back to our true purpose.

"I remember Django complimenting M Moreau on his bakery, saying that you could taste his heart in every baguette! In fact, he joked that we should send deliveries of bread to Germany, that Moreau's bread would melt the stoniest of hearts." Mme Moreau was still lost in her memories.

"Well, I think we have our answer right here," Johnny said, looking at us all as though we were blind. "Django Reinhardt, one of France's best loved musicians, came to his cousin's bakery during World War II to play an impromptu concert for the locals and declared Moreau's the best baguette in all of France. I mean, you couldn't make up a better marketing campaign!"

"Really?" asked Mme Moreau, looking doubtful.

"Of course! Do you have any idea what a big deal that is? Especially for musicians like me," he said. "It's easy, all we have to do is put some photos up, maybe display an old guitar and the story of the night he played here."

"Actually, you might be onto something there," I said, picking up the thread. "This friend of mine, Geoff, he's a tour guide and he would love any story that connects to the war. He could bring all his ex-pat tours here!" I was so pleased because, despite my misgivings, we actually had something of a plan.

"Unless, you don't want us taking advantage of your connection to Django?" I said to Mme Moreau, just in case we were getting ahead of ourselves. I knew how much she guarded her privacy.

"Are you kidding? That cheeky musician won money from my father plenty of times playing billiards. He was not shy about making money and I think he would be happy to help out his little cousin," she smiled. "I love the idea."

"And if you like, I could play here at the weekend, create a bit of an atmosphere," Johnny suggested.

"I'll set up a Twitter account," said Nicole, equally enthusiastic at the prospect.

"Right, well it looks like we have a plan – operation Django is go!" I roared, and we all raised our glasses.

***

We all had our jobs to do the following week and I started by revisiting the printers and designing new flyers to give to Geoff and the local hotels and tourist office. I was able to find an old photograph online of Django Reinhardt playing guitar with his crippled hand – which was quite remarkable. He sported a thin little moustache and sleeked back hair. He had a mischievous look about him, just as Mme Moreau had said and she was delighted to see her long lost cousin helping to bring new customers to her bakery. I found a beautiful antique frame at the market and had another photo printed out to hang in the shop, just beside the front door. Johnny sourced a very old-looking guitar that we hung behind the counter and just below it, I hung a poster detailing the events of the night Django Reinhardt played at La Boulangerie et Pâtisserie de Compiègne.

I felt such a renewed sense of optimism about our plan, that I was sure the bank would change their minds about the bakery's future. I struggled to write up some sort of a business plan, but when it came to the projections, I really had no idea what to put. Despite my hopefulness, there was no way to predict what would happen or how the public would respond to our ideas. All I knew was, Mme Moreau could not be kicked out of her home – she could not leave her father, and Manu's future was riding on our plan's success.

Still, there was one issue I couldn't fix; Hugo. Seeing him in the bakery that day was so unexpected. I thought he had come to surprise me; take me out to lunch or ask me to dinner. I never imagined for a moment that he was part of the problem that was pushing Mme Moreau out of her home. Even though I didn't like admitting it to myself, I had quietly been building up my hopes and expectations around him. I had never felt that way about anyone before, and even though our time together was short, I was able to open up to him in a way that came so natural to me. Now, that only felt like a betrayal. And that should have been enough for me to turn my back on him, but I couldn't.

I checked out Chadwick Holdings online and discovered that Hugo Chadwick had only held the position of CEO for six months. He had said that his father died 15 years before, so I started to wonder why he had only taken over the company now. Their website was a tribute to sterile buildings of glass and chrome, boasting high yields on investments with an international portfolio. It just didn't add up. The man I met and even sang to on a bench beside the river that night was deceptively shy and spoke at length about his love of photography. His boyish charm convinced me that he had the heart of a bohemian beating beneath his tailored suit.

Walking back to the bakery and armed with flyers, posters and little black and white postcards that Johnny thought might sell, I almost tripped over him as I turned the corner.

"Hugo, what are you doing here?" I said, trying my hardest to sound displeased at his presence.

"Can I help you with your things?" he asked politely but without smiling.

"No thank you, I can manage fine on my own. Besides, I don't think you'd be welcome inside, do you?"

"Just give me the opportunity to explain Edith, you can give me that much at least," he said rather forcefully.

I considered it and figured there was nothing to lose by hearing him out.

"Just let me drop these inside," I said rather coolly.

***

We walked to a café near the main square and sat at a table outside. The day was fine and bright, if a little chilly. When the waiter served us our coffees, I looked at Hugo expectantly.

"How are you?" he asked, again with a strained politeness.

"How am I? You asked me here so you could explain yourself. Explain!"

"Right, okay, straight to the point then."

"If it's not too much trouble."

"Edith, like I told you, my father passed away some years ago. His brother, my uncle, took over the family business after that and grew it up into the company it is today."

"You must be so proud," I said with a saccharin smile.

"I know what you must think Edith, but you're wrong.."

"Oh I'm wrong now, am I?" I interrupted and got up to leave, but he grabbed my hand.

"Please, just let me finish."

I sat back down and nodded for him to continue.

"My uncle, he's taken ill and it is his wish that I take over the reins. I never wanted anything to do with the business. My father's plan was that I should succeed him, not my uncle, but I couldn't do it. I was never the son he wanted me to be; I let him down. I ran away and well, let's just say our differences were never resolved." He had been stirring his coffee up to this point, but now he gulped it down as though it were brandy. "Now the company needs a new leader and I have to step up to the plate, Edith. I can't let my father down again; I can't ignore my responsibilities any longer."

148

There were so many things I wanted to say, but the one thing that kept bugging me was why he concealed the truth

"Why did you lie to me? You told me you were a photographer and when you walked me home, you knew that I lived and worked at the bakery. How could you have kept all this from me?" I suddenly realised that I was talking as if I was his girlfriend and felt my cheeks begin to burn. "I mean, I know we don't owe each other anything, but the least I had hoped for was the truth.

"I never meant to lie and I didn't lie about the photography. After my father's death, I spent years travelling around Europe with just my camera for company. It gave me a reason to get up in the morning and to keep moving every day – trying to find the next great shot. I got pretty good at it too. But it's not exactly a career, is it? No, I wasn't going to fluff my responsibilities at the second time of asking," he said, shaking his head.

"Is that your father talking or you?" I said, without really considering the power of the words. His features changed dramatically and I suddenly wished I could take the words back.

"I see, I get it. You come to France hoping to 'find yourself' in some shitty bakery just to make yourself feel better about your life and you judge me for trying to run a successful business? Face it Edith, the bakery is going to default and Mme Moreau would be much better off accepting our offer and finding a nice little flat outside of town somewhere. Oh no, but you'd prefer to take the moral high ground and see her end up on the street when the bank fore-closes, is that it?"

I was shocked into absolute silence. I couldn't believe he could be so hurtful and cruel and I could feel the tears start to sting my eyes as I got up to leave.

"Don't worry, I won't stop you this time," he said, looking down at his feet.

"Well thanks for explaining your motives Hugo," I said, my voice trembling, "you've made things a lot clearer for me."

I walked away and as soon as I turned a corner, the tears began to fall.

Chapter 22

Nothing was really working out as it was supposed to. I lay in bed that night, thinking of all the expectations I had when setting off on that flight from Dublin to Paris. I had well and truly lost my way in life and that was long before my mother's passing. Although I was too ashamed to admit it to myself, I had used her illness as an excuse to avoid my own life. Every time someone suggested that I try something different or go somewhere new, I always had the excuse of caring for my mother. Not that I regretted that time, but I could have been there for her and lived my life at the same time. Cystic Fibrosis had forced my mother to see life as one big opportunity that has to be grabbed and enjoyed before it's too late. I admired her for her courage and wanted so much to be like her. But life doesn't work that way.

Without realising it, I took on the role of being my mother's little nurse. I doubt she realised what was happening either, or she would have booted me out of the house and sent me to boarding school. But our bond was so strong and as I got older, I found there wasn't really any time left over to think of myself and in a strange way, that helped. If my purpose in life was to look after my mother, then I didn't have to explain to anyone why my own life was so empty. Looking back, I could see that I never gave myself time to grieve, or acknowledge what was really going on. I distracted myself and everyone else with endless tasks and things to be done. The reality was just too difficult to accept. 'What will we do without her? How will we keep on living?' They were the kind of questions I couldn't ask my father at the time and so instead, I either buried myself in the practicalities, or escaped in a marathon of black and white movies. The well of grief is deep and I was afraid I would drown in sorrow if I ever acknowledged its presence. But just before her death, my mother sat me down and made me face the inevitable.

"I don't want to leave you and your father, Edie, we've had such a happy life together. But that's what I want you to focus on; how lucky we were to have had this wonderful time as a family. We've got to be grateful for that. Otherwise, you'll spend the rest of your life full of bitterness and resentment and I don't want that for you," she smiled, brushing my hair from my face with her soft, porcelain hands.

"But I am bitter!" I said, "It's not fair…" I said, then buried my head in her lap, crying all of the unshed tears that had stored up over the years. She had soothed me then, like she had countless times before, saying that no, it wasn't fair, in a voice that made resignation seem like the right thing to do.

"I can't lose you," I said finally.

"You'll never lose me Edie," she said smiling, "I'm in here," she said, tapping my chest.

Her words gave me courage to carry on, but it didn't stop me missing her. I still wished I could be back there now, watching an old film with her and rhyming off the lines we knew by heart. I needed a friend. Picking up my phone I texted Nicole and asked her if she had ever seen The Wizard of Oz. It was a bit late for such random questions, but she said she hadn't, so I suggested a DVD with Max the following evening and she enthusiastically agreed.

***

The next morning I began baking and frosting my cupcakes as usual and placed them on a tiered stand on the counter. They looked so bright and cheery and to my delight, sold out rather quickly. One remained when Manu came back from school for his lunch and he happily gobbled it down in three large bites.

"Is going well, no?" he asked, pointing to the empty cake stand.

"Yes," I agreed, "but it's still not enough to help our business proposal. I'm going to meet Geoff now and see if he can bring some tourists our way." No sooner had I said the words when Geoff and Ruby arrived with Little and Large.

"Hello guys!" I greeted, fussing over the dogs who rewarded my efforts with sloppy wet kisses on my cheek.

"They love making new friends," said Ruby, who had them both sporting little fleece-lined jackets to protect against the chill.

"So, how can we help?" said Geoff, getting straight down to business.

I brought them inside and hung up the closed sign on the door for lunch. I made us all some coffee and served them some warm croissants with butter and jam.

"So, you know I really enjoyed your tour the other day, visiting the Armistice clearing and the site of the old internment camp," I said, "and I was wondering if you might consider bringing some of your tours here?"

"We could do that, of course" he nodded, looking to Ruby for agreement, "I'd be happy to bring them back here for refreshments. Mmm, by God, you can't beat a warm croissant straight from the oven!" he said, licking his lips.

"Yes, they are strangely addictive," I agreed.

"Only thing is," Ruby interrupted, "a lot of those history buffs might not be that interested in coming back into the town for coffee, most of them just hop back on the motorway or the train and back to Paris."

"Yes, but what if they were coming to visit the house where Django Reinhardt played during the war? The bakery where his cousin now lives and works?" I held my breath, hoping they would be interested.

"You don't mean here?" said Geoff.

"I do indeed," I said, rather smug.

Just then Mme Moreau appeared, as if on cue, and the dogs rushed to greet her.

"*Oh, bonjour mes petits*" she cooed, obviously a dog lover.

"Mme Moreau, you remember Geoff and Ruby Harding?"

"*Ah oui, M et Mme Éclair*!" she joked affably and shook their hands.

"Well, Geoff runs a tour guide business," I continued, "and he might be interested in bringing his tours here," I said, beaming with pride.

They all embraced warmly and Mme Moreau sat down to discuss the details with them. She still wasn't comfortable talking about the loss of her parents to the camps in Germany, but Geoff was so experienced in the area that he made it a little easier for her. However, she became highly animated when talking about Django and his visit to the boulangerie that night.

"Well it was during the war and of course with the curfew, it was quite dangerous, so M Moreau was worried for our safety. However, Django had that charming way about him that seemed to make everyone forget about the war, just for that night. And so the word quickly spread of our little soiree from shopkeeper to shopkeeper, housewife to housewife. They decided to set up an impromptu concert in the basement, where no light or sound could be seen or heard from the street. The locals quickly shuffled through the side door that led down the stairs and into our candle-lit basement, where I had helped my mother set up some chairs and tables. I remember it so well, for it was the last time I saw my mother dance. I can hear it now; her heels click-clacking on the

154

flagstones, the laughter of our neighbours, all enjoying themselves for that one, fleeting moment. Even M Moreau clapped along to the playful plucking of the guitar. Django entertained us until very early the next morning. I was very young and grew tired quickly, but I would not let myself fall asleep – even when my mother sat me on her lap. I just let my head loll on her shoulder as we swayed along to the Minor Swing."

Geoff and Ruby were enthralled. The dogs had lapsed into something of a coma at our feet and before I realised it, it was almost time to open up again and I had a batch of cake pops to prepare.

"So, what do you think?" I asked, abruptly breaking the spell Mme Moreau's story had cast. "I've got some flyers printed up here that you could hand out to people," I said, passing them to Geoff.

"What a story, eh?" he remarked, clicking his tongue against the roof of his mouth. "I thought I knew all there was to know about this place in World War II, but this is a really interesting snap shot."

"I'm afraid you're all going to think me a fool, but I've never heard of Django Reinhardt," said Ruby apologetically.

"Oh don't feel bad," I said, "I hadn't heard of him either before I came here. Tell you what, I can give you his cd, I think you'll really enjoy it."

I was delighted with their response and Geoff's willingness to make the boulangerie one of his tour destinations. He reckoned Mme Moreau's story had something for everyone, although I couldn't help but think how he would react if I told him about M Moreau's nightly presence in the basement. No matter how well intentioned these people were, we couldn't risk telling anyone about the ghost in the basement. The only possible outcome of such a revelation would be mockery or worse, a downpour of ghost hunters landing on the doorstep, neither of which would help Mme Moreau.

***

That evening I set off to Nicole's house with a copy of The Wizard Of Oz I'd found on a market stall. I was glad to get away from the bakery for a while. I realised that I was doing the same thing I always did; burying my head in plans and schemes to avoid my true feelings, so I knew I needed time off to get some perspective. It was clear I had made the right call, when, snuggling up on the couch with an over-excited Max gnawing on my white chocolate cake pops, my heart soared with joy. Seeing him experience the magic of the Emerald city, Dorothy and her faithful friends for the first time was extremely special. He didn't make it to the end of the movie, which was just as well because I never liked the flying monkeys when I was a child and I wasn't sure how he would react. His heavy head slung over Johnny's shoulder as he put him to bed, no doubt dreaming of tin men and scarecrows and Toto the dog.

Nicole opened a bottle of wine and I let her pour me a very large glass.

"We've got over 100 followers on Twitter," she said, pouring herself a glass and tucking her legs under her.

"Oh that's good," I said, munching on some pistachios she had placed in a bowl.

"Well, don't get too excited," she said, looking at me strangely.

"Sorry Nicole, no that's great, really. I just, can I be honest?"

"I would be offended if you weren't," she said frankly.

"I just hadn't planned on taking on a 'cause', you know? That's not why I came here."

"You're afraid of ending up like Jeanne d'arc?"

"Joan of Arc? Hardly. Although remind me, what happened to her in the end?" I asked, slightly embarrassed at my lack of knowledge when it came to French history.

"She was captured in this very town."

"You're kidding! Joan of Arc was in Compiègne? Is there anyone who hasn't been to this place?!" I joked.

"It's true, France had girl power long before the Spice Girls," Nicole smiled. "You must have seen her statue in the main square?" she asked, shaking her head.

"Oh that's who that is," I said, sounding like the worst tourist in the world.

"Yes, she totally kicked ass and led France to victory in many battles. However, she was captured by the Duke of Burgundy and the English army right here, while she was attempting to save Compiègne from invasion. They burned her at the stake for heresy, but later she was made a martyr. Now she is a patron saint of France."

"A martyr and a saint? Yeah, no. That's not exactly what I had in mind when I came here," I replied.

"Do you mind me asking, why did you come here Édith? I don't want to be nosey, but I didn't buy your story really," she said in her candid way.

I took a large gulp of wine and tried to be brave enough to share my real story with Nicole.

"My mother died a year and a half ago, and after years of putting my own life on hold, I wanted to honour her memory by living the life she gave me." Saying it quickly kept the tears at bay.

"Oh Édith, I am so sorry – you poor thing," she said, embracing me warmly.

"It's okay, we always knew her time was limited, so we just got on with it. But, ever since she… passed away, I've just been sort of lost… and drifting. So I did something completely out of character and I thought that by coming here, I would just shock myself into waking up and finding out who I am or what I want to do, I suppose. I think I used her illness as an excuse to avoid my own life. But now she's gone and I don't know who I'm supposed to be." I was slightly embarrassed at baring myself like this, but the wine helped and there was something about Nicole that made it seem okay to not have things worked out.

"So now you find yourself trying to save a bakery and take on a French bank, when all you wanted was a change of scenery?" she summed up.

"Yes, something like that. I mean, I really like Mme Moreau and I'd love to be able to help, but it's all become a bit much."

"Hmmm," she nodded, pouring more wine. "What about Hugo, have you heard from him?"

I realised that I hadn't even had time to tell her about what happened at the weekend.

"You're not going to believe this – he is the head of the company that are bidding to buy the bakery and turn it into a hotel," I explained, even though she baulked at the idea.

"You cannot be serious? How is that possible?" she asked, marvelling at my spectacularly bad luck in love.

"Oh I'm serious alright. I met him with his estate agent at the bakery. The worst part is that I thought he had come to see me. I was sure I could convince him somehow; get him to see how important the bakery is to Mme Moreau, to the community."

"*Attend, attend.* Forget about the damn bakery for a minute – what about you and him?" she questioned, putting her two forefingers together.

"There is no me and him, not now," I said, feeling pretty glum. "He crossed a line."

"Ah, now I see why your spirits are so low."

"He said some really nasty things; like how my life is just so boring that I had to come over here to try and 'find myself', as he put it." I was still fuming at the thought of his insolence.

I noticed Nicole quietly smirking to herself and, despite my reservations about her oftentimes brutal honesty, I asked her why.

"This is just what you said to me, about why you came here. It sounds as if he read you like a book and you're upset because he said it."

"That's not the point," I argued, despite the fact that her argument made perfect sense, "it's the way he said it." I was a little surprised; I just assumed that she would take my side, but as I was coming to learn, French people speak their minds no matter what. She was still smiling.

"Anyway, it doesn't matter. His company is still going to go ahead with the purchase, unless I can convince the bank not to foreclose."

"Maybe, but it's not over till *la grosse femme* sings, right?"

"Right," I said, knocking back the rest of my wine.

"And remember ma belle, you are not on your own. Just as Jeanne d'Arc had her army, you have friends here and we're going to fight with you to the end. *Jusqu'au bout!*" she shouted, raising her glass.

"*Jusqu'au bout!*" I repeated, clinking our glasses together.

Chapter 23

Time had not made living in a haunted bakery any less spooky. Every night before bed, I found myself wedging a chair against the door, despite the fact that everyone knows ghosts can quite easily pass through walls. Even the wine didn't help me to sleep that night, as I tossed and turned thinking about the presentation of our business plan to the bank the following day. Of course I couldn't go – partly because my limited French wouldn't lend itself to a financial meeting with the bank manager, but mostly because I wasn't a stakeholder, just an employee. Manu was too young and so it was left to Mme Moreau to convince the bank that we had a plan to increase the bottom line and the means to service the loan. I despaired of our chances, because while Mme Moreau was very business savvy in the bakery, her presentation skills were non-existent. And as for me, my employment background left quite a deficit when it came to preparing a business plan for a sole trader – in French. I downloaded a template I found online from an Irish website, but I had no idea if this would translate to what a French bank would be looking for.

At some point during the night, I found myself on trial, surrounded by a lot of angry faces shouting at me in French. They seemed to be blaming me for something, but I couldn't quite make out what exactly. 'No, you've made a mistake - I'm not Joan of Arc!' I kept pleading, but it was no good. A line of red macaroons with gargoyle faces led me to the stake, where the fiery flames licked the wooden logs and cake pops chanted 'burn her' in unison. I woke up from my confectionary nightmare, screaming my innocence. The dark, empty room just stared back at me, finally convinced of my lunacy. I refused point blank to risk falling back into that weird dream, so I gave up on sleep and tottered downstairs for a hot chocolate, just as I had done all those weeks ago when I first 'met' M Moreau. I almost tripped over myself with fright when I saw Manu sitting at the counter.

"Jesus, you frightened the life out of me!" I cried.

"*Desolé* – sorry," he said.

"What are you doing down here? Do you want a hot chocolate?" He shrugged and decided it couldn't hurt. I put on some milk to boil and got out the packet of marshmallows from the cupboard. I had a feeling our chat would require marshmallows and cream. When I presented him with his drink, he smiled gratefully and bobbed the marshmallows into the cup with his finger.

"*Ça va?*" I asked.

"I don't know. If we are not successful tomorrow, maybe we lose the shop, our home too," he sighed.

"Look, I'm worried too but we've got to be positive," I said, more out of instinct than anything else. I didn't want to give the boy false hope, but what else can you say?

"*Merci Édith*, for all your help," he said, raising his cup to me.

"*De rien*," I said, "I'm hardly Joan of Arc am I?" I joked, my psychedelic nightmare still fresh in my mind.

"You gave grandmère hope again… and me too. Sometimes it was *difficile* to live with the secret – of great-*grandpère*. Grandmère, she does not trust many people, so when you came, well, *tu as tout changé quoi.*"

"Well, I hope I've changed things for the better, but we won't be sure till tomorrow," I said. "But listen Manu, no matter what happens, you are such a talented apprentice. Please promise me you will build on M Moreau's legacy?"

He nodded, quite satisfied with the compliment, then checked the time and decided he should get downstairs and start the ovens.

"It's nice to have someone young here too, you know?" he added, gulping down his drink.

I couldn't remember the last time someone had referred to me as being young and in that moment, it made the whole enterprise seem worthwhile. Although, given the age gap between himself and Mme Moreau, I suppose anyone under sixty would have seemed young to Manu. "I'll come with you," I said, somewhat hesitantly. "We'll let your grandmother lie in – she has a big day today."

***

Despite my own misgivings, working with the hologram that was M Moreau, was not the terrifying experience I feared it would be. In fact, there was something reassuring about his presence there – a timelessness that made you feel as though life could carry on, regardless of all the change in the world. Still, I did my best to tip-toe around the general area where he (I want to say stood, but his feet never actually touched the ground) worked. It was hard work, filling the mixing troughs with flour, mixing the water and yeast at just the right temperatures. For a skinny teenager, Manu wrestled the dough like a prize fighting champion, pounding it into submission. I floured all the tins and kept an eye on the fire, adding logs when necessary. It was really quite moving to see the two bakers working side by side and it brought a tear to my eye to think that they had never met, not properly anyway, but still shared this family legacy.

162

If only I could have told people about this; they would have been queuing around the block. But it was impossible and just as Mme Moreau had said, he would not be there for much longer. I noticed his light flicker and go out a little sooner than the last time I was there. I could sense Manu's disappointment when he turned around to me and said, *"Il est parti,"* in a resigned tone.

We opened up the shop and after Manu left with the deliveries, I coped quite well with the morning's brisk trade. Mme Moreau came downstairs just before nine, wearing a dark navy skirt and jacket and a bright string of pearls at her neck.

"Bonne chance!" I shouted after her, as she made her way primly out the door. I could see she was anxious; their entire future rested upon that meeting and I quietly prayed to God it would go her way. Still, there wasn't much time to brood. At around eleven, Geoff passed by the window with about a dozen tourists in tow. My heart soared, watching him gather them in like wayward sheep.

"We've come for our packed lunches wench!" he called from the door. "It's such a beautiful day, we've decided to have a good old-fashioned picnic in the woods," he told me and said his group were more than happy to pay top dollar for our artisan bread. "They want an authentic French picnic, so load her up darlin'," he said, presenting me with a giant wicker basket.

I proceeded to cut thick slices of rustic baguettes and stuff them with pâté or cheese as required. While I placed the tasty-looking sandwiches along with some Pâtisseries in a picnic basket, Geoff held court in the middle of the floor and eloquently told the story of Django Reinhardt's visit to Compiègne and his connection to the proprietor, Geneviève Moreau. They lapped it up and gazed inquisitively at the large framed photo of the gypsy guitarist behind the counter. I mouthed a very big thank you to Geoff and was rewarded with that nonchalant wink of his that said, nothing is a problem.

"I'll be bringing another tour in the evening for coffee and a bun, so save some cupcakes for me, won't you love?"

"I will be your own personal cupcake factory if you keep bringing in the punters like this!" I beamed. For the first time, I really believed we could make this work. Then Mme Moreau returned.

***

"I can't believe it," I repeated for the hundredth time. "Did you show them our projections?" I could see that Mme Moreau was weary from answering my questions, but I did not cease in asking them.

"I told you Édith, it is just a drop in the ocean. I have been missing my payments for some time now, and these projections will only cover the interest on the loans. They want a lump sum now, before they will even consider a restructuring of the loans."

It seemed unthinkable, but I felt that Mme Moreau was not as upset as I was about the news.

"You look like you're just giving up," I said.

"And what would you have me do, Édith, chain myself to the door and refuse to sell?"

"Well, yes! Where is your fighting spirit?" I asked.

"I'm old Édith, and I'm tired. I don't want to fight anymore. They are offering me a little apartment in the suburbs. At least Manu and I will have a home" she said, slipping off her leather court shoes and climbing the stairs.

My heart sank and all of my hopes with it. The more I thought about it, I started to wonder if it wasn't the bakery I was trying to save, but myself. I just couldn't let it go. I texted Nicole with the news and she replied with a simple "I'm on it". I had no idea what she was on, but I hoped it would happen soon.

Chapter 24

Saturday morning heralded another visit from Hugo. He wore a black suit with a black mac flying open like a villain's cape behind him. I was serving coffee to two little old ladies who always stopped by with their teeny tiny dogs for some sweet treats and a gossip. Like a saloon in the wild west, the shop went deathly quiet when he entered, save for one of the little dogs who barked like a Rottweiler – clearly perturbed by the evictor's presence.

"Good morning Edith," he greeted me in that deep tone that made my skin prickle. But I was not going to be won around that easily - I was still smarting from his sharp tongue.

"Is it?" I replied.

"I wondered if I might speak to Mme Moreau," he asked.

"I'm afraid she's taken to her bed with a headache, but then, being evicted from your home will do that to you."

"I wish you wouldn't put it like that," he muttered.

"Oh really, well how would you like me to put it Mr. Chadwick? Tell me please because I'd hate to offend your sensitive disposition." My temper was rising and I no longer felt in control of what I would say to him.

"Well, it's not like we're putting her out on the street is it? We are offering her perfectly adequate accommodation elsewhere," he said.

"You're too kind," I grimaced.

"Look, I came here to inform her that we have moved ahead with our purchase of the vacant premises next door.."

"What?" I was completely shocked at this revelation. "Are you planning on buying up the whole street?"

"Not exactly, but we will be knocking through to next door and creating greater floor space for the bedrooms, with a larger reception area downstairs." He seemed rather pleased with this summation of building works.

"How on earth did you get planning for that? This is a listed building," I argued, even though I wasn't entirely sure what that meant.

"Oh we're retaining the original exterior," he sniffed.

There was something about him that didn't ring true. He shifted uncomfortably and fidgeted with his tie. It took one to know one, I thought.

"You don't agree with this, do you?" I asked, trying to read his expression. After several moments of silence, during which the old ladies whispered something to each other in French, he erupted again.

"Look, this is happening whether you like it or not. Now I know this bakery is your little 'project', but my company is going to make a real success of this building and bring more tourism to the area. So just tell Mme Moreau will you?" he snapped.

"Is that how you usually get what you want Mr. Chadwick, by bullying people and shouting out orders? Because I can tell you right now, I'm not giving in without a fight" I threatened.

"Don't you mean 'we'?" he said, with something approaching a grin on his face.

"Yes, that's what I said; we." I was fuming with him and his know-it-all attitude. But most of all, it was the way he could read me like a book that made me furious.

"Very well Miss Lane," he concluded, "I look forward to our duel, but just to let you know, I usually win" he said, looking intrigued at the idea of taking me on.

"Just so you know, I don't play fair," I said, bemused by my own words, as if I were speaking lines from a movie. He bowed theatrically and left the shop with a grin on his face.

"What the hell did I say that for?" I said to the ladies who, despite the language barrier, seemed to understand that our quarrel was not strictly business.

***

It was true. I read the letter Hugo had left for Mme Moreau and even with my limited French, I could understand that Chadwick Holdings had purchased the building adjacent, with plans to knock through and build a sizeable hotel. I gave the letter to her that evening, after we had closed the shop.

"Well, it is finished then. They would not have invested so much in purchasing the building next door if they did not intend to have this building too." She rubbed her eyes and looked away from me.

"You can't give up Mme Moreau, there must be some other way," I pleaded, but I could see my supplications were falling on deaf ears.

"Edith, you are a kind girl, but I do not have the money; it is as simple as that."

"I've heard that 'kind girl' routine all my life, but you know what? I think you're confusing kindness with weakness. I might not look it, but I've got guts and I'm not afraid to use them! These faceless investors think they can just come along and buy their way into a piece of history, without a thought or care for the people they are trampling over, just to make a profit. And it seems to me as though the bank is in cahoots with them. I mean, they didn't even give our proposal a chance!" I ranted.

"Listen to me, I am just an old lady with an old bakery and a lot of debt. You cannot blame them for everything; I must take responsibility also."

"But that's just it; you are taking responsibility and we can turn things around, if they'd just give us more time.." I broke off. I could see she was tired and that my ravings were only exhausting her even more, so I decided to head out for a walk in the cool night air to clear my head. I called my Dad and explained the situation.

"I hate to say it Edie, but it sounds like a fait accompli," was his response.

"Fait accompli? When did you start learning French?" I was surprised.

"Well I have to practice for my trip, don't I?"

A moment or two passed before his words sunk in. "You're coming here? That's brilliant news!" I said, realising how wonderful it would be to see a familiar face.

"You can thank your Aunt Gemma - she's had me plagued to book the flights since the moment you left," he chuckled. "So we'll be seeing you in Frogland sometime soon."

"Please don't call it that when you get here!" I begged. "Still, you better make it sooner than later or I might be gone home myself."

***

I woke up to the sound of chanting and had to sit myself up on my elbows for a moment to try and remember where I was. I looked at the room, at my now familiar settings and shook my head, but the chorus of voices was still there. I stepped out onto the cold floor in my bare feet and tip-toed towards the window facing onto the street and drew back the curtains. When I opened the window, the wall of sound that hit me almost knocked me backwards.

"*Sauvez notre boulangerie! Sauvez notre boulangerie!*" The cacophony of voices rang out in the morning air, catching the bemused glances of passers-by. A gathering of about 40 people stood outside the door to the boulangerie with placards of varying messages ranging from 'Down with capitalism' to 'Save the local baguette'. Leading the chants were Nicole and Johnny, equipped with tambourines and a large drum, beating out their message like a tattoo. I never felt so inspired in my life and ran to pull some clothes on.

"*Qu-est ce qui ce passe*?" Manu asked, emerging bleary eyed from the basement, his eyes adjusting to the bright lights.

Mme Moreau followed behind him, looking at the waiting crowd outside with some confusion.

"Who are these people, Edith? What are they doing here?" she asked.

"They're saving the bakery!" I cried happily.

I ran outside and fell into Johnny and Nicole's arms.

"You two are completely nuts, you know that! Where did you find these people?"

"I told you I was on it," said Nicole triumphantly. "I put the call out on Twitter and Facebook - told everyone that our local traditional bakery was being closed by the bank."

Johnny butted in, "Everyone's sick of being burned by the banks and if there's one thing the French are good at, it's protesting."

"Exactly, so the whole thing sort of snowballed," Nicole continued. "We're expecting a gang of students from the university in the afternoon."

"I... I'm speechless Nicole. Thank you so much for doing this," I said, kissing them both.

I wasn't sure what kind of effect this little protest would have on our banking friends, but at least it was going to raise awareness of Mme Moreau's plight. When I came back inside, I saw her looking rather stern.

"They've come to help," I said.

But she simply turned around and went back upstairs.

"What's wrong with her?" I asked Manu.

"You can understand, she is ashamed that everyone will know about our problems," he said quietly.

I bit my lip and turned again to see the small crowd chanting loudly and moving in a slow, circular procession. Maybe it was a tad over the top.

"You stay here and open up, I'll go and talk to her," I said, as I ran up the stairs two at a time.

When I got to her apartment, I noticed that the door was left ajar. I stepped cautiously in and saw Mme Moreau clutching the photograph of herself and M Moreau, taken outside the shop.

"It was his ambition that I should take over from him," she said gently. "He never had any children of his own and he considered me like his own daughter."

I edged close enough to see the smile on both of their faces in the sepia toned image.

"I didn't mean to upset you, Mme Moreau. To be honest, this wasn't even my idea, but people want to help."

She looked at me then. "I hardly know the people down there, why are they here but out of pity."

"It's not pity, I promise you. It's support. I know it's hard to accept help, especially from people you don't know, but they're doing this because they want to stand up for what's right. Just like M Moreau stood up for you and your mother that day at the train station."

I hoped I wasn't crossing a line with her, but I desperately wanted her to understand how much the place meant to everybody around here.

"Besides, I think you'll find you know quite a few of these protesters, just come to the window and have a look."

We looked out onto the street below and saw Nicole's mother Jacqueline, the two old ladies with their dogs yapping, the couple who owned the crêperie, the Algerian man who ran the tabac and many of the boulangerie's regulars – all of Mme Moreau's vintage, shouting and clapping and demanding justice.

"*Mon dieu*!" she cried, clutching her hand to her heart.

"You see? People care about you and the bakery and they don't want you to leave. So what do you say; are you going to disappoint your customers?" I realised that was what I should have said at the start, for it was like a battle cry to her.

"The Moreaus never disappoint their customers!"

I followed her down to the bakery, where she immediately set about handing out complimentary croissants, *pain au chocolats* and drinks to the crowd. This raised everyone's spirits and voices and even Manu took the day off school to keep the momentum going. It was like a party atmosphere outside the shop, which only served to drive more customers in, which in turn led to greater publicity about the foreclosure. I was so swept up in the euphoria, that I hardly noticed Hugo weaving his way through the crowd.

"A protest, how very original," he sneered in my ear, close enough for me to feel his breath on my cheek.

"Play it cool all you like Chadwick, but I would chalk this up as a victory for the bakery," I replied, rather smug.

"A handful of students with a drum? I'm literally quaking in my boots," he said, deadpan.

But just then, I noticed a mini bus pulling up at the end of the road, and out popped Geoff, Ruby and about twenty other people, who marched up towards us with more placards and whistles. Even Little and Large tagged along.

"I think you may have underestimated us Mr. Chadwick," I smiled, noticing the grimace on his face.

"Look Edith, I really wish you would reconsider this whole thing. The truth is that you're only prolonging the agony for Mme Moreau and her grandson, because this deal is going through no matter what. I don't want to be the bad guy here, but if it wasn't our company taking over the property, someone else would. The bank doesn't care who they sell to."

For a moment I saw a glimmer of the man I had first met, but it was too little too late. Battle lines had been drawn and he was on the wrong side.

"You don't get it do you? The reason we're all standing out here freezing our bits off is because we're trying to show Mme Moreau how much the bakery means to us. These kinds of independent, artisan bakeries are closing down every day and pretty soon, there'll be no more left. Maybe you'd prefer a homogenised high street with Starbucks and McDonalds, but these people, they value their heritage and Manu – he is the future of this place. His skills have been handed down through generations-" I faltered, thinking of how present his ancestor really was.

"Fine, carry on. I can see you won't be reasoned with," he concluded.

"Wait," I said, before he turned to leave. "Why not try one of our croissants? It might help to get my point across," I said, placing it in his hand.

He took a bite, but as always, his expression was unreadable and he turned away, disappearing into the crowd.

Chapter 25

By the following week, Nicole's Twitter campaign to save the bakery had gone viral. Artisan bakeries from all over France pledged their support to Mme Moreau and it seemed that her individual story had sparked something of a national debate. Even celebrities were hopping on board, insisting that France needed to retain its cultural identity in the face of globalisation. No one was more stunned by the response than I was. Frankly, it was a little overwhelming. All I wanted to do was help Mme Moreau to keep her home and her business for Manu, but now the protestors were talking about descending on Paris and the Minister for Food and Agriculture to demand more support for small businesses.

It was Friday night and, as planned, Johnny and his band came to the bakery to play some Django Reinhardt tributes. The floor space was impossibly small, but a nice crowd managed to cram their way in. I hoarded a box full of jam jars and lit candles in them all over the shop, which created a lovely atmosphere. As the music began to play, I could see Mme Moreau's face light up for the first time since I had arrived.

"He is good, this Johnny, *hein*?"

"He's passionate," I replied, admiring his love of the gypsy style of playing.

"He has *la duende*," she remarked with a wink.

The crowd clapped and cheered for more after every song and I wondered if this is what it felt like on that night during the war. The music was hypnotic and defied anyone not to move or sway to its rhythmic beat. If only this place was bigger, I thought to myself, we could really make a go of this. We had no liquor licence, so everyone brought their own bottle of wine, but we served platters of bread, cheese and cold meats.

"There's a great atmosphere, isn't there?" I said to Nicole as I squeezed back behind the counter.

"That might be about to change," she said, nodding towards the door.

I couldn't mistake his tall silhouette, his lean build or his piercing blue eyes.

"Shit," was all I could say. Not because he was the enemy or that he might be bringing us more bad news, but because I hadn't done my hair in ages and at the moment it was scraped back into an unflattering pony tail. Why wasn't I wearing my new red dress? Instead I was in my usual black blouse and skirt with my pink polka dot apron. It wasn't exactly a power suit or an outfit to stop traffic in.

"You're blushing Eddie!" Nicole whispered.

"It's just hot in here," I assured her, trying to hide behind the counter. Johnny and his boys wrapped up another swinging number by Django Reinhardt, 'I'll see you in my dreams' and the small audience clapped their appreciation. I could hear a voice shouting something beyond the hubbub and everyone else stopped their cheering in order to hear.

"Let's hear Miss Lane sing a song," came the taunting words from the door, then repeated in French for everyone else's benefit. Heads turned in search of this elusive Miss Lane and people asked each other if anyone knew of her.

"Eh, that's you Eddie," Nicole pointed out needlessly. "Why is he asking you to sing?"

Johnny, in his enthusiasm, shouted at me to join him on the imaginary stage.

"Come on Edith, give us a song!"

My head now resembled a well-roasted beetroot. "No, no" I replied, "I'm not a singer" I assured everyone, while my nails dug into the counter.

"*Au contraire*," the goading voice came again, "you told me you were a singer – and I'm sure the lovely lady wouldn't tell a lie," he smiled mischievously, like the villain in a pantomime, entertaining the crowd. It had the desired effect, for the audience assumed that this was an act, that I would feign reluctance only to turn around and belt out a heart-warming number like Édith Piaf. They all clapped, including Mme Moreau, Manu and Nicole. There was no way of backing out and he knew it.

I smiled graciously at the audience and took my apron off. They all cheered supportively and I made my way, jelly legs and all, over to Johnny and his band.

"You're a dark horse!" he said.

"You haven't heard me sing yet," I whispered out of the corner of my mouth.

"So, what will it be Miss Lane?" he asked, returning his guitar.

The first song that came to mind was 'Cry me a river', but I didn't want to give Hugo the satisfaction of thinking I had shed any tears over him. "I'm a fool to want you," I said, with my tongue firmly in my cheek.

"Oh, I love Billie Holiday's version of that," said Johnny, as he began discussing keys and arrangements with the guys, while I stood looking out at the expectant crowd.

It was one of those moments when you think to yourself, how the hell did I end up here. I could feel Hugo's eyes upon me and saw his Cheshire grin from across the room. He was calling my bluff and was probably going to make a fool of me in front of all these people. Correction, I was going to make a fool of myself, he just instigated it. Once again I found myself in a moment of intense fear, and once again I prayed to my mother for help.

"One, two, three, four…" counted Johnny and I took a deep breath.

Think Billie Holiday, I whispered to myself; slow, relaxed and sultry. I opened my mouth, closed my eyes and began to sing:

I'm a fool to want you; I'm a fool to want you
To want a love that can't be true
A love that's there for others too
I'm a fool to hold you, Such a fool to hold you
To seek a kiss not mine alone
To share a kiss the devil has known…

I lost myself in the song and the words and by the last verse, I was actually enjoying myself. Despite my complete lack of confidence, I knew that I was somehow captivating the audience. Perhaps it was the song, or the story I was telling, but I believed it and I knew they did too. It was my first time singing with a live band and I relished every second of it. Instead of hearing myself a capella, my voice was supported by a soft snare drum, a deep resonating bass and a rhythmic guitar. When I sang the last line, I finally dared to look over where Hugo had been standing. He was leaning against the door, his head cocked to one side and a sly grin on his face. Our little gathering of people erupted into wild applause when I stopped singing and I was showered with kisses and shouts for an encore. For the first time in my life, I felt as though I was doing what I was always meant to do. It felt natural and just… right. I saw the door opening and Hugo's tall frame exiting and it was only then that I realised he had done me a favour. Perhaps he wasn't trying to humiliate me after all. Maybe he was giving me a shot at my dreams. I extricated myself from the embraces of my new-found fans and ran after him out onto the street.

"Why did you do that?" I shouted.

He turned around in that debonair way he had that meant he never looked as though he was in a rush.

"I wanted to hear you sing."

"No, you wanted to prove your point; that I had lied about being a singer just as you lied about being a photographer," I panted, out of breath after my impromptu performance.

"Why would I do that?" he said, leading me.

"To prove we're both as gutless as each other when it comes to living our dreams," I replied. He just smiled, like a cat toying with a mouse.

"The only difference is, I'm not a very good photographer, while you..." he broke off.

"Sorry?" I asked sarcastically, "Was that almost a compliment?" We were both smiling at each other, which made a nice change to our recent encounters.

"Why are you being nice to me now?"

"I never wanted to be not nice Edith. It's this place that came between us," he said, gesturing to the bakery.

"Well, I still can't see a way around it," I said and we both fell silent for a time.

"I see your protests have reached Paris," he said, "I saw an article in Le Monde. You're really not going to give up, are you?" He looked at me in a strange way, as though he begrudgingly admired my tenacity.

"If you knew what this place meant to her Hugo, you wouldn't give up either. If I could only tell you..."

"Édith!" came Manu's voice, just in time. "*Ils veulent un encore*," he shouted.

At this, Hugo bowed slightly and said, "Your audience awaits Mademoiselle." With that, he took his leave and it took all of my willpower not to call after him.

The cheer that welcomed me as I came back in almost floored me. It couldn't all be pity, I told myself. They really wanted to hear me sing again.

"Why didn't you tell me you had those pipes?" Johnny said, as I re-joined him and the guys.

"I wasn't sure they'd work outside of the shower!" I shouted over the noise.

"Fancy giving it another go?"

I nodded, almost afraid to voice my overwhelming desire to sing all night. Like a latecomer who's hidden their light under a bushel for so long, I wanted to shine. I sang a little French song by Melody Gardot, aptly called '*Les étoiles*', the stars.

***

Finally, it was time to call it a night and after we thanked our patrons and sent them home, I began cleaning up. I felt a little like Cinderella after midnight, returning to her day job. I stacked the chairs up onto the tables and mopped the floor, while Mme Moreau totted up the receipts at the cash register.

"Why do you think Mr. Chadwick stopped by this evening?" she said after a time.

"I've no idea," I replied, applying myself to an imaginary stain on the floor.

"He seemed to know that you were a singer," she remarked, almost casually.

I couldn't think of a reply, so I just kept my mouth shut and hoped she'd forget about this line of inquiry.

"I think he likes you."

"What? Don't be ridiculous," I blustered.

"I think you like him too," she continued, sounding not altogether displeased with her revelations.

"Well it wouldn't matter anyway, I mean it's not like anything can happen between us." I kept mopping and she kept prodding.

"Why not? You're single, he's not married…"

"Eh, hello? I said, leaning the mop against the counter. He is our nemesis, remember? He's shutting down the bakery? How could I possibly love a man like that?"

"Love, eh?"

"Oh you know what I mean," I said exasperated.

"Édith, how many times must I remind you, it is the bank that is closing us down. Mr. Chadwick, he is just a business man hoping to buy a premises at a good price."

"You mean a vulture picking at a carcass," I said under my breath.

"Is that what you truly believe? Or is that what you're telling yourself, so you can avoid the feelings that are obviously shared between the two of you."

If it had been a game of chess we were playing, this was checkmate. I confided in her about how we had met, that magical night and then the terrible arguments we had over the bakery. Not to mention the hurtful things he had said about my life here.

"It's natural ma belle, you care about what he thinks of you," she said gently. "But just think; maybe he cares about your opinion of him also," she pointed out.

I remembered then how I had accused him of bowing down to his father's expectations. Perhaps I had touched a raw nerve of his also. It was obvious he felt guilty about letting him down.

"And if you ask me, I think he went out of his way to put things right tonight, *n'est ce pas*?"

180

Chapter 26

On Sunday, I took myself off to the Château Compiègne for a walk around the grounds. A fresh breeze set the grass swaying like a Van Gogh painting, making everything feel alive and full of energy. Once again, I found myself in awe of its grandeur and wondered what life must have been like for its occupants. I walked the long avenues that led onto the forest; the perfect place for reflection and contemplation. So much had happened since my arrival in France, not least my singing debut the night before. I felt like I really needed to think about what I was doing here and whether there would be any point in staying on if and when the bakery closed. Despite all our efforts and the public goodwill, the final say still rested with the bank and they didn't have any emotional attachments to the building – only the desire to balance their books.

Hugo had touched a nerve that day when he said I was coming here to find myself. It was such a cliché, but clichés are only so because they are true. Life was passing me by and I had never had the courage to put myself out there and find my dreams. I didn't even know what my dreams were, until last night when I sang for that little gathering in the bakery. I could feel an unfamiliar sensation running through my veins and all I knew was that I didn't want it to stop. Still, I knew nothing about the music scene here, or back home in Ireland for that matter. Could I make a living out of it? Or even a hobby that might make a boring day job seem worthwhile? Was I good enough? These were all questions I couldn't answer, but it felt like a huge step forward, finally knowing the right questions to ask. It felt as though I was getting to know myself a little better. Which made me wonder; what would my mother make of this new career choice? That was still the hardest part about missing her. I wished I could just ask her things like I used to; run my ideas by her. I wondered if her spirit, like M Moreau's, was trapped in a video – doomed to play itself over and over again. Or if her spirit was out there somewhere, conscious and able to hear my thoughts? I preferred the latter and without thinking about it, found myself talking to her. I chatted as though she were right there with me, like we used to do at the kitchen table back home over a cup of tea. I told her all about the bakery, Mme Moreau and my conflicting feelings towards Hugo.

By the time I got back home I felt lighter and happier. I picked up some groceries on the way at the *supermarché* and rang Aunt Gemma to talk about her upcoming visit. We agreed that she and my father would book the flights and I would get a good deal on a nice hotel here. I rang off full of the joys and hopped up the stairs to my apartment, just as evening was setting in and turning the sky from pale blue to a soft amber glow. As I turned the key in the lock, I noticed a red envelope just tucked under my door. Bending to pick it up, I saw that it was addressed to Miss Lane in a familiar script. Inside was an invitation that read:

You are cordially invited to dine at
No. 21 Rue St. Antoine
This evening at 7.30pm

I flipped the card over, but no more information was forthcoming. I leaned against the door jamb for a moment, trying to figure out what was going on. That was the vacant building next door that Hugo's company had bought to convert and merge with the bakery building, in order to create a larger hotel. I couldn't understand what it was all about. Suddenly, I jerked myself out of my thoughts and realised that it was nearly six o'clock. I was still standing in the doorway dressed in jogging pants and sporting four-day-old hair. I rushed into my little apartment; switched on the immersion for a hot shower and hung my red dress in the bathroom to get the creases out.

By 7.15pm, I had finished straightening my hair and was brushing the side parting to the left like Nicole had shown me. I put on some red lipstick and pressed powder on my face with a puff. A little dab of Chanel behind my ears and I was ready to go. One last look in the mirror showed me a shapely woman with something approaching joie de vivre. I was no longer the frumpy spinster at the bus stop watching the world go by – I was a frumpy spinster living her life and it felt good. I realised I didn't need to be like everybody else, I just needed to be me.

Mme Moreau was out at Sunday evening mass and Manu was over at a friends', so all was quiet as I stepped carefully down the stairs in my high heels. I had wrapped a shawl around my shoulders, but I still had goose bumps, either from the chill or the anticipation. I walked out of our door, locking it behind me and took three steps to the left. Number 21 was also a timber-framed building and while I had passed the burgundy wooden door plenty of times, I never really noticed it before. Now, the door was open, with a dark velvet curtain obscuring my view. I pulled the curtain aside and peered into the dimly lit room. Once my eyes adjusted, I could see a table at the far end of the room with a candelabrum lighting the corner. Then I saw him, sitting patiently and waiting for me to come in.

"What are you doing here?" I asked. "What's all this about?"

"Good evening to you too," was the reply. "Would Mademoiselle care for a glass of Champagne?" he asked, getting up to pull out the other chair. "That is some dress," he added admiringly.

I felt slightly hypnotised by the whole thing. It was ridiculously romantic and he looked simply ravishing in a black dinner jacket and open white shirt. I felt so flattered, but my integrity tugged at me like a persistent child. I couldn't let myself be swayed so easily. A sweet female voice sang in hushed tones from a stereo in the corner, creating a seductive atmosphere.

"You're not going to change my mind with all of this you know," I said, taking my seat. "Who is that singing by the way?"

"Stacey Kent, I thought you'd like her. In fact, her voice reminds me of you," he said. "You sang beautifully last night," he added, as he poured the Champagne.

He couldn't possibly have known how much that compliment meant to me, but even so, I did my best to conceal my pleasure. It was then that I noticed a silver cloche on the table and when he lifted it, I was surprised to see a pepperoni pizza.

"Pizza? Very posh," I smiled, finding it harder and harder to fight his charms. I decided that the best means of defence was attack, and so I pestered him about the building.

"What was this place before you bought it, do you know?" I asked, looking around the space.

"I think it used to be a shoemaker's at some point. I found a last upstairs," he said, taking a bite of his pizza.

"You mean a cobblers," I corrected.

"No, a shoemakers. A cobbler repairs shoes."

"God you're infuriating!"

"Why? Because I say things as they are?" he asked, slightly confused by my reaction.

"It's the way you say it, like you know everything and the rest of us are idiots."

"Well I can't help it if you feel that way," he explained, still quite calm in the face of my bluster.

"Look, why am I here anyway? Do you want to rub my nose in it or something?"

"Rub your nose in what?"

"Ooh, I don't know, the fact that you're so rich you can just snap these kinds of places up and eradicate years of history so you can turn them into some sterile, money making investment?" I couldn't believe I was arguing with him again. It seemed to happen on the turn of a sixpence.

"Actually, if you'd let me explain..." he began, but I was already getting up from my seat.

"Hugo, I don't want to argue with you, but this is hopeless. We're never going to agree," I told him straight. "Thank you for dinner, though." I walked towards the door, but in the gloom, tripped over something hard and ended up splayed out on the floor.

"Edith? Edith, are you okay?" Hugo called out.

"Oww!" I groaned, as I held my arm up to assess the damage.

"Hang on, I'm coming …. Woah!" Hugo shouted, as he landed rather ungainly on top of me.

"Oh God, I'm so sorry," he began. "Are you hurt?"

"It's okay, I don't think I quite broke all my bones with the first impact, so thanks for that," I said, panting under his weight. I could barely make out his features in the gloom, but his scent filled my head, while the warmth of his body spoke a language that mine clearly understood. Before I knew what was happening, my lips had betrayed me and met his, hungrily. It was as though I had forgotten everything that had just happened and my mind was clear. Everything was Hugo.

186

His hands reaching for every part of my body, his lips in a race to do the same. I could feel my skin craving his touch, as we fumbled blindly to free each other of our clothes. After several run-ins between my hard edges and the cold cement floor, I eventually came to my senses.

"Wait, sorry, I can't," was all I could manage, as I tore myself away from him and scrambled to my feet.

"No, I shouldn't have... But hang on, I haven't had a chance to tell you!" he pleaded, but I was already out on the street and opening the door to the bakery. I ran up the stairs and let myself into my apartment, leaning against the door behind me as I tried to catch my breath. My lips curled into a smile despite my best efforts to resist the attraction between us. I simply couldn't trust myself around him anymore. I was already making great plans to avoid him in future, when I heard him calling my name out on the street.

"Edith, please, we need to talk!" he shouted.

I stood motionless for a moment. I realised that Mme Moreau was right. I was afraid. My feelings for him were overwhelming and it frightened me to death.

"Edith, I can stay out here all night you know," he yelled. "You know how annoying I can be."

I was finally able to move towards the window, which I opened out wide.

"Will you come down?" he asked.

"You'll have to speak to me from there," I said, trying to arrange my features into that of a mature woman in control of her senses.

"It's rather private."

I just shrugged.

"Fine, have it your way Miss Lane. What I was trying to tell you, if you had given me half a chance, is that Mme Moreau will not lose the bakery."

He stood awaiting my response, but I just leaned on the window frame, staring at him agape.

"You'll catch flies doing that you know."

"I'm coming down," I called and almost did myself another injury taking the stairs at speed. I ran out into the lamp lit street and saw him there, casual as anything, leaning against a lamppost.

"What did you say?" I panted.

"I said, the bakery will not close. I've spoken to the board and convinced them that investing in the business as a going concern is a much better option. What's more, we plan to convert number 21 into a jazz bar and restaurant – a far better return than the hotelier business."

I was still confused.

"Hang on, are you saying that you're still going to buy the bakery, but you're not going to turn it into a hotel?"

"No, not buy. Invest," he said, pupils enlarging with pleasure at my reaction. "I'll run through the details with Mme Moreau tomorrow, but I wanted to tell you tonight."

"So, what, are you a philanthropist now?"

"God no, don't let the board hear you say that! But let's just say I've figured out a way to make Chadwick Holdings a bit more ethical," he replied, looking pleased with himself.

"I don't believe it, what made you change your mind?"

He moved closer to me and bent his head slightly, so his lips almost touched my earlobe.

"You really need to ask?" he said, as he kissed me softly on my neck. "It was that croissant, best one I've tasted in years," he said, smiling.

Chapter 27

I woke up in the middle of the night, wrapped in Hugo's arms. Tempted as I was to stay there and fall asleep, I could see from the alarm clock in his hotel room that it was almost four o'clock, and I knew Manu and Mme Moreau would be up soon. He woke up just as I was pulling on my shoes.

"Where in God's name are you going at this hour?" he croaked, with one eye open.

"I just have to tell Mme Moreau the good news," I whispered.

"Why are you whispering, there's no-one else to wake up," he pointed out.

"Ah yes, I see you're just as fastidious in the morning," I said, kissing him on the cheek.

"But it's not morning," he argued, trying to pull me back into bed.

"I can't, I have to tell her, you've no idea what it means," I said excitedly.

"I think I do."

***

"*C'est un miracle!*" she kept saying, while she hugged Manu and myself until we could hardly breathe. As the elation began to die down, I noticed something.

"Wait a minute, where is M Moreau?"

They both exchanged regretful looks; then Mme Moreau turned away.

"He only appeared for a few seconds," Manu explained. "It was different this time. His light burned so brightly, like a kind of golden glow, like never before. Then... nothing." He glanced over to where Mme Moreau was standing, arranging some bread pans.

I walked over and put my hand on her shoulder.

"He's gone," she said in a very small voice.

"How do you know?" I asked.

"I just know."

All of a sudden, the basement felt very empty.

"But why now?" Manu asked.

Mme Moreau wiped some tears from her eyes. "Perhaps he knew that the bakery would be saved," she pondered, "maybe he didn't need to stay anymore."

I searched desperately for some words of comfort, but what could you say to someone who was mourning the loss of a ghost? Then I remembered something I read on the Internet about souls not being able or willing to move on.

"I think you're right," I said, linking both of their arms. "I think M Moreau's instinct to protect you was so strong in life, that he could not let go of his role in death. That's why he kept coming back, night after night. But now, we all have each other and the future of the bakery is safe, so maybe he can finally let go of you, Geneviève." It was the first time I had used her Christian name, because it seemed a bit too formal at this stage to be calling her Mme.

"Group hug?" Manu suggested.

"Where did you learn that?" Geneviève asked him curiously.

"I've learned a lot of English listening to you two chatting all of the time," he said smiling, and we all hugged.

Epilogue

After several months of banging, drilling and general construction noise, number 21 opened its doors as Compiègne's new jazz bar and restaurant. I helped Hugo with a lot of the interior design, choosing colours and accessories. We painted the walls a pale grey colour and hung large photographic prints of all the jazz greats; Louis Armstrong, Ella Fitzgerald, Duke Ellington, Billie Holiday and of course, the infamous Django Reinhardt. It was an eclectic mix of the old, original features and art deco furnishings. The restaurant was situated upstairs, with reclaimed tables and chairs painted off-white and downstairs the bar was fitted with dark grey velvet booths and soft blue sconces on the walls.

On opening night, we all gathered outside for the unveiling of number 21's new name. Mme Moreau was chosen for the task, and as she pulled the material from the sign above the door, the name 'Django's' glowed in silver letters.

"Do you think he'd approve?" I asked her.

"I think Django would be happy as long as the music is loud and the wine keeps flowing," she laughed, looking splendid in a royal blue dress with a pink pashmina.

We all piled in for a look at the finished product. In the far left corner, where I had sat with Hugo for dinner all those months ago, was a stage with Johnny's band belting out an upbeat version of Glen Miller's 'In the mood'. The staff moved efficiently between tables, sporting buttoned up white shirts and black suspenders. I could hardly believe that the empty old building had been transformed into something so vibrant and welcoming.

"Where is Hugo anyway?" Nicole asked, looking hot as ever in a sprayed-on dress in canary yellow. "I want to thank him again for giving Johnny's band a residency here. He really needed a break like this – I thought we were going to have to move to Paris for his music, but thanks to Django's we can stay in Compiègne."

"I'm not sure, he might be up in the office," I shouted over the music. "I'll go have a look." I climbed the back stairs to the top floor and sure enough, found Hugo poring over some documents.

"What are you doing? The party is downstairs you know," I said.

He kissed me, a little longer than was entirely necessary, before showing me some papers.

"There's a problem with one of the contracts," he said, looking worried.

"What do you mean?"

"I'm afraid that, if you don't sign on this line, Django's could be in real trouble," he said.

"What are you talking about?" I asked, a little bewildered.

He handed me the contract, which stated in no uncertain terms that I was to sing at the club at least one night per week, after my duties in the bakery of course, accompanied by the house band.

"Are you kidding me? You actually had a solicitor draw this up?" I asked in disbelief, seeing the headed paper.

"Well I had to. Otherwise you would have done your whole modest; 'I'm not a real singer' routine and I really didn't have the patience for that. So, are you going to sign or not?"

I sat down on the leather office chair behind his desk and took in the scene.

"Hugo Chadwick, what happened to that corporate shark, intent on turning a profit and making a pound of flesh for his investors?"

"I think we both know that was not a role I relished. When my father died, I saw my future mapped out in front of me; a future I never wanted, but I just didn't know how to deal with it. So I escaped and found a way to avoid everyone's expectations, including my own. But when I met you, I found a kindred spirit. Only you refused to remain a victim to your circumstances. You're the most frustrating, determined woman I've ever met!"

It was hard to believe that he was actually talking about me, Edith Lane, scaredy cat extraordinaire!

"And yet you retain this wonderful innocence..."

"Naïveté you mean," I cut him off, slightly embarrassed by this barrage of praise.

"No, I know what I mean. Your integrity was so refreshing; especially in my world and so I suppose you could say that you inspired me to face my demons head on. That's when I came up with the idea for the bakery and this place," he said, looking about him.

I sidled up to him and began playing with his tie.

"You know you had me at '*Bonjour*'," I said coyly.

He put his arms around my waist, pulling me closer.

"Oh I think I had you long before that," he said, "probably from the time you spotted me at the bar," he grinned.

"Ah yes, there's that old arrogance I fell in love with," I replied, realising too late that I had said 'love'.

He must have seen the look on my face and seized his opportunity.

"It's not your fault Edie, you can't blame yourself for falling in love with me," he mocked, then pulled me close to him and did that thing where he brushed his lips ever-so-lightly along my neck. "I love you too, you silly woman, that's why I want us to move in together – that's if you can bear to leave your teeny tiny attic in the sky," he said.

"But you live in a hotel," I said, completely missing the point.

"Yes, well I thought I could sell my apartment in Paris and buy something here. What do you think? Or would you rather live in the city of light?"

"Really Hugo," I said, "when you've got all of this, who needs Paris?"

The End

###

About the author

Evie Gaughan is the bestselling author of The Heirloom, The Story Collector and The Lost Bookshop under the pen name of *Evie Woods.*

Living on the West Coast of Ireland, Evie escapes the inclement weather by writing her stories in a converted attic, where she dreams of underfloor heating. Her books tread the intriguing line between the everyday and the otherworldly, revealing the magic that exists in our ordinary lives and the power of an individual's determination to inspire change.

Described by The Irish Times as having a writing style that *reads with the warmth and charm of a fairytale,* Evie is currently working on her fifth novel.

Join the mailing list for exclusive updates on Evie's upcoming books. You can also follow Evie on her Blog, Twitter and Facebook.

Made in the USA
Las Vegas, NV
03 February 2024

85235309R00114